THE SECRET AT THE HERMITAGE

Books by

CAROLYN KEENE

Nancy Drew Mystery Stories

The Secret of the Old Clock
The Hidden Staircase
The Bungalow Mystery
The Mystery at Lilac Inn
The Secret at Shadow Ranch
The Secret of Red Gate Farm
The Clue in the Diary
Nancy's Mysterious Letter
The Sign of the Twisted Candles
The Password to Larkspur Lane
The Clue of the Broken Locket
The Message in the Hollow Oak
The Mystery of the Ivory Charm
The Whispering Statue
The Haunted Bridge
The Clue of the Tapping Heels
The Mystery of the Brass Bound Trunk
The Mystery at the Moss-Covered Mansion
The Quest of the Missing Map
The Clue in the Jewel Box

The Secret in the Old Attic
The Clue in the Crumbling Wall
The Mystery of the Tolling Bell
The Ghost of Blackwood Hall
The Clue in the Old Album
The Clue of the Leaning Chimney
The Secret of the Wooden Lady
The Clue of the Black Keys
The Mystery at the Ski Jump
The Clue of the Velvet Mask
The Ringmaster's Secret
The Scarlet Slipper Mystery
The Witch Tree Symbol
The Hidden Window Mystery
The Haunted Showboat
The Secret of the Golden Pavilion
The Clue in the Old Stagecoach
The Mystery of the Fire Dragon
The Clue of the Dancing Puppet
The Moonstone Castle Mystery
The Clue of the Whistling Bagpipes
The Phantom of Pine Hill

The Mystery of the 99 Steps

Dana Girls Mystery Stories

By the Light of the Study Lamp
The Secret at Lone Tree Cottage
In the Shadow of the Tower
A Three-Cornered Mystery
The Secret at the Hermitage
The Circle of Footprints
The Mystery of the Locked Room
The Clue in the Cobweb
The Secret at the Gatehouse
The Mysterious Fireplace
The Clue of the Rusty Key
The Portrait in the Sand
The Secret in the Old Well

The Clue in the Ivy
The Secret of the Jade Ring
Mystery at the Crossroads
The Ghost in the Gallery
The Clue of the Black Flower
The Winking Ruby Mystery
The Secret of the Swiss Chalet
The Haunted Lagoon
The Mystery of the Bamboo Bird
The Sierra Gold Mystery
The Secret of Lost Lake
The Mystery of the Stone Tiger
The Riddle of the Frozen Fountain

The Secret of the Silver Dolphin

THE SECRET AT THE HERMITAGE

By

CAROLYN KEENE

Grosset & Dunlap, *Publishers*
NEW YORK

CONTENTS

▼

"Louise," cried Jean, "Come here and see what I've found."

The Secret at the Hermitage

"Louise!" cried Jean. "Come here and see what I've found!"

The Secret at the Hermitage

CHAPTER I

MISTAKEN IDENTITY

"LOOK at this, Louise."

Jean Dana, blonde, and inclined to be boyish, was sprawled upon the cushions of the window seat, reading the headlines of a newspaper spread out before her.

"Better put away that paper and do a little work on your French," advised Louise, her pretty, dark-haired sister. "I suppose you're trying to improve your mind with the comic sheet!"

The two girls were students at Starhurst School in Penfield. Classes were over for this afternoon, and the sisters were in their own study. Jean at the moment was preferring the newspaper to a textbook. It was a mystery to Louise how her sister stood so high in her classes for she spent as little time as possible with her assignments.

1

"Oh, we've both done enough studying for one day," Jean insisted carelessly. "Do come and read this item. Harold Norton has broken into print again."

"What has he done this time?" Louise crossed the comfortable studio room to peer over her sister's shoulder.

The man was known to her only by hearsay. She vaguely recalled that a year or two before he had lost his position as warden of Pinecrest Reformatory through some scandal which had swept the state.

"Norton says in this interview that he never received an honest deal," Jean declared. "He announces he's not going to rest until he gets his old job back."

"He may be pretty tired before he's through, then," Louise commented dryly. "If what folks said was true he never gave the prison inmates half enough to eat."

"That's the trouble with this place," a gay voice cut in. "They don't give us enough to eat."

The Dana girls turned to see Evelyn Starr standing in the doorway. Without waiting for an invitation, she selected a cushion and established herself in the other corner of the window seat.

"If you're hungry, have a cookie," Jean invited, jumping up to get a box from the table.

"Aunt Harriet sent them today and they're delicious."

"I'm always hungry," Evelyn admitted, greedily selecting the largest piece of pastry.

She was an attractive girl, a staunch friend of both Jean and Louise. In turn they admired her for the courageous way in which she had accepted misfortune.

Years before, the fine mansion which housed Penfield's exclusive school for girls had been her own luxurious home. Through various causes the Starrs had lost their money. One piece of property after another had been sacrificed. When Evelyn's fortunes were at their lowest ebb, Jean and Louise had been helpful. Through their clever efforts the girl had recovered a valuable cache of jewels. She had not forgotten the kindness.

"I really shouldn't stay," Evelyn announced when she had finished her cookie. "I have lots of work to do. What time is it?"

Louise looked at her wrist watch and noticed that it had stopped running. She took it off and tried to wind it. The stem turned freely without tightening the spring.

"It seems to be broken," she said in alarm. "Oh, dear, Uncle Ned gave me that watch for my birthday."

"Let me see it," Jean requested. "Probably the spring is broken."

"That's what happened to my watch once," Evelyn contributed. "It doesn't cost much to get it fixed."

"I don't know what I'll do without a time-piece," Louise complained. "I sleep and eat by that watch."

"Why not take it to town this afternoon and have it repaired?" suggested Jean, always eager for an outing. "Mr. Growler, who runs that interesting little shop down town, could do it for you."

"I'd like to go along," Evelyn added. "I need a new fountain pen. Besides, Mr. Growler's shop is exciting. He has everything imaginable stuffed away on his dusty shelves."

"I like to hear the man talk," Jean confessed, twisting her features to resemble those of the grumpy, eccentric shop owner.

To the amusement of Evelyn and Louise, she mimicked him perfectly.

"All right, let's go," Louise decided. "If we start in ten minutes we can catch a bus."

"My hat is in Doris Harland's room," Jean cried. "I'll get it and be back in a jiffy."

She flung open the bedroom door and, darting out, ran full force into a girl who was coming up the hall, her arms filled with books. Two of the volumes fell to the floor.

"Oh, I beg your pardon," Jean apologized.

The Briggs girl, not a popular student at the

school, glared at Jean as she hastily reached down to recover the books; a trifle too hastily, it seemed to Louise and Evelyn, who had witnessed the incident through the open doorway. Their curiosity aroused, they sauntered into the hall. The older Dana was quick to note the unusual cover and title of one of the volumes.

"I should think you might watch where you're going!" Lettie was saying crossly to Jean.

"I told you I was sorry. I didn't damage the books, did I?"

"You probably have loosened the bindings," Lettie said irritably. She loved to make a great ado over trifles, and was now in a quarrelsome mood.

"Let's see if I did." Jean reached out to take the volumes but Lettie drew them back. She had no intention of permitting the other girl to see what she had been reading.

"You must expect to do a lot of studying tonight," Evelyn commented innocently. "Are all those textbooks?"

"Every one," Lettie said glibly.

Louise glanced at her sharply. She disliked people who told untruths.

"How about that gaudy-looking book of fiction I saw you pick up?" she asked significantly. "If I am not mistaken, the title is 'Prison Walls.'"

Lettie's sullen face flushed; yet she eyed Louise brazenly.

"Well, what of it?"

"Nothing at all," Louise retorted sweetly. "I don't doubt but that you have a natural and deep interest in prison inmates."

The shot went home. Not so many months before Lettie had been deceived by someone who had been sentenced to prison following his conviction as an international spy. The students laughed about it behind Lettie's back.

"Oh, you make me tired!" With that feeble response, Lettie fled down the hall, doubtless to seek the consolation of her faithful shadow, Ina Mason.

"Perhaps I shouldn't have said what I did," Louise remarked. "Only it annoys me when anyone tells falsehoods."

"You certainly squelched her," Evelyn chuckled. "For a minute I thought she was going to choke."

Jean ran to an adjoining room for her hat and the girls hurried off to catch their bus. While they were waiting at the corner, an automobile drove by, a woman at the wheel.

"That's Mrs. Grantland," Jean exclaimed, waving frantically.

The car slowed down and stopped a little farther on. The girls ran to greet the driver.

"Are you on your way to town?" Mrs.

Grantland inquired pleasantly, opening the car door. "I'll give you a ride."

The girls accepted the invitation with alacrity, explaining their mission. The pleasant woman was fond of the Dana sisters, and frequently took them for drives in the country or to a matinee. She declared that it was little enough to show her appreciation for all that Louise and Jean had done for her in solving a mystery.

"I can drop you off at Mr. Growler's shop if you like," she promised. "But if you're not in too great a hurry I should prefer to have you stop at my home for a few minutes first. I have something to show you."

During the drive to Mrs. Grantland's attractive house she talked enthusiastically of her latest hobby—the accumulation of choice pieces of statuary. The girls listened politely, though in truth without a great deal of interest. Their attitude underwent a remarkable change when Mrs. Grantland actually led them into a salon where she kept her many art treasures on display.

"This is what I wanted to show you," she announced, indicating a small marble statue which occupied the place of honor in the room. "It is called 'The Recluse.'"

The piece was unusual both in design and subject, obviously the work of a gifted artist.

As far as the girls could determine, it was a representation of a hermit in long flowing robes who stood with arms uplifted. The sad expression on his face held them silent for many minutes.

"You like it," Mrs. Grantland beamed in delight. "I knew the instant I saw the statue that it was out of the ordinary. And it has such an interesting history."

Eagerly the girls urged her to explain.

"I don't know the name of the sculptor," Mrs. Grantland admitted. "Or rather, it has slipped my mind. But the statue was made by a prisoner at Pinecrest Reformatory."

Louise was looking at the base of the figure. In it were cut two tiny initials, N. R. She showed them to Mrs. Grantland.

"Strange, I never noticed the marking before," the lady said in surprise. "I suppose they are the initials of the sculptor. I wish I could recall the name."

The girls spent a longer time than they had intended in admiring the many fine statues. It was growing late when Mrs. Grantland finally drove them to Mr. Growler's shop.

"Shall I wait for you?" she asked.

"Oh, no," Jean thanked her. "We'll take a bus home."

The store owner was about to lock the door when the girls hurried inside. Another man, obviously a latecomer like themselves, stood close by conversing with the shopkeeper.

"Folks say harsh things about me," the customer declared. "But what I told you is the truth. I'd still be warden today if that honor prisoner hadn't escaped two years ago. It made my record look bad. If I ever catch Nina Regan——"

Louise and Jean turned to glance at the stranger. They recognized him now as Harold Norton, ex-warden of Pinecrest Reformatory, whose picture had appeared in the afternoon newspaper.

The man was a hard-faced individual, older than the girls had imagined him to be. The lines of his face indicated that he was at least sixty. He was dressed in severe black, and wore a large felt hat which partially hid his features. Being near-sighted, he squinted as he turned to gaze at the three girls.

"Good afternoon, Mr. Growler," Louise said pleasantly. She suddenly became confused and could not go on. The ex-warden was staring at her as if he had seen a ghost. It was embarrassing.

She was destined to be even more humiliated as Harold Norton suddenly sprang forward and clutched her by the arm.

"Nina Regan!" he cried triumphantly. "I've captured you at last!"

CHAPTER II

A Significant Initial

Louise was so startled at the unexpected accusation that for a moment she could say nothing. Then she jerked her arm free, regarding the ex-warden coldly.

"You have made a mistake, sir. I am not Nina Regan."

"I'd know your face anywhere," the man told her triumphantly. "Even in that schoolgirl disguise, you can't fool me!"

"You're—you're near-sighted," Jean broke in furiously, trying to push in between the two. "That's why you made the mistake. I never heard such a ridiculous accusation."

"My name is Louise Dana. I can prove it."

"You'll do your proving at the police station."

"Don't you dare try to take my sister to jail!" Jean cried.

"You've made a mistake," Evelyn Starr added. "Louise attends Starhurst School for Girls."

With three against him, the ex-warden wavered. He even wondered if he had made a mistake.

10

"Better have a care what you're doing," the shopkeeper warned with a sardonic smile.

That smile goaded the ex-warden beyond endurance. He could not bear to appear stupid in front of Mr. Growler, especially as he had been boasting only a few minutes earlier of his ability in identifying criminals. Determined to see the thing through, he clutched Louise by the arm again, and pushed the girl roughly toward the door.

Jean and Evelyn made a dive for Norton. He tried to shake them off, but they clung. In the scuffle a glass jar was knocked from one of the counters. It fell to the floor with a loud crash, splintering into a dozen pieces.

"Stop it! Stop it, I say!" Mr. Growler shouted, wringing his hands. "You are wrecking my shop!"

He ran to the door, and seeing a policeman at the corner, yelled for him to come. The officer stopped the commotion by threatening to use his billyclub over the ex-warden's head.

"What's the trouble here?" he asked, eyeing Norton suspiciously. "What are you doing to these girls?"

"They fell on me like a pack of wolves when I tried to take this escaped convict back to jail. I guess you know me, Officer. I'm Warden Norton."

The name carried weight despite the fact that

the man had left office under a cloud. Louise and Jean tried to explain their side of the case. The policeman scarcely listened to their story.

"You'll have to go to the station," he told Louise.

Jean would not desert her sister, and Evelyn, too, was intensely loyal. When the police car arrived they climbed in beside Louise and the ex-warden. The policeman rode on the steps, his arms stretched across the exit, for all the world as if his passengers were dangerous criminals. It was humiliating; especially when a small group of curious pedestrians gathered to see what was going on.

"There's Lettie Briggs!" Jean hissed, trying to duck down out of sight. "Don't let her see you, Louise."

The warning came too late. Lettie, who had emerged from a candy store, was staring open-mouthed at the police vehicle. A pleased smile illuminated her homely features. What a story she would have to relate when she returned to Starhurst!

"We'll never hear the last of this," Louise groaned.

Lettie and the Dana girls were enemies of long standing. Jean and Louise had tried to be generous, but they could no longer ignore the many mean and cutting tricks played upon them by the spoiled girl.

Lettie disliked the Danas intensely because they were popular, and because they stood high in their classes. She could not forgive the manner in which they had exposed an acquaintance of hers to the authorities. The girls' clever detective work in this connection has been recounted in a recent volume of the series, "A Three-Cornered Mystery."

As the reader has learned in "By the Light of the Study Lamp," Louise and Jean were orphans who lived at Oak Falls with a maiden aunt, Harriet Dana, and her brother, Ned Dana, captain of the transatlantic liner *Balaska*. Louise, seventeen, was a year older than her sister, and inclined to be more serious. Both girls loved adventure and always welcomed an unusual experience. However, a ride to the police station was not their idea of the right kind of excitement.

"Don't you care," Jean whispered comfortingly into her sister's ear. "We'll soon have everything cleared up."

It was not as simple as she predicted, however. First there was a lengthy wait before they were ushered into the presence of the police judge. It became increasingly clear that the ex-warden had prejudiced court officials against Louise.

Nina Regan, they learned as the ex-warden presented his case, was a notorious character.

The young woman, a seamstress, had been convicted of setting fire to the home of her employer, a Mrs. Henriette Keating, who unfortunately had burned to death. Robbery was the motive for the crime. A large sum of money and valuable jewels had been found in Nina Regan's possession. Since she was an orphan, there were no relatives to help her fight the case. Though she staunchly maintained her innocence, the seamstress had been sent to prison for a long term of years. Thirteen months after she had been placed in Warden Norton's custody, she had escaped.

"Ever since then I've been searching for her," the man declared. "I recognized her instantly when she stepped into Mr. Growler's shop."

"Let me see." The judge consulted a stack of records which had been brought to his desk. "Nina Regan was thirty-one years of age at the time she was sentenced to Pinecrest Reformatory."

He looked keenly at Louise and grew perplexed. Not by any stretch of the imagination could one believe that the Dana girl was out of her teens.

"She's fixed herself up to look younger," the ex-warden interposed nervously.

"I think your eyes have deceived you, Mr. Norton," Louise declared. "If I remember correctly, it was partly on account of failing eyesight that you were relieved of your duties as warden.''

"Norton, you've made a ridiculous mistake,'' the police judge snapped. "Case dismissed.''

"Then are we free to go?'' Louise asked in relief.

"Yes,'' the officer told her, "and I'm very sorry that you and your friends were caused so much annoyance.''

On the steps outside the police station the girls paused for a consultation. They felt that their afternoon had been ruined. Now it was too late to take Louise's watch to the repair shop, even had they cared to return to Mr. Growler's place of business.

"I suppose we may as well go back to Starhurst and face the music,'' Louise said in deep disgust. "Probably by this time Lettie has spread the story everywhere.''

"No, let's return instead to Mrs. Grantland's house!'' Jean cried unexpectedly.

"But we were just there,'' Evelyn protested.

"Why do you wish to see her again so soon?'' Louise queried curiously. From the look of subdued excitement in her sister's eyes she suspected that Jean had a worthwhile reason.

"Because I want to look at that statue again, Louise.''

"You mean 'The Recluse'?"

"Yes, I just thought of something that Mrs. Grantland told us about it."

"That it was made by a prisoner at Pinecrest Reformatory," Louise guessed, sensing the trend of her sister's thought.

Jean nodded.

"And Louise, don't you remember something else? A matter of deep significance, it seems to me."

For a moment Louise was puzzled. Then an answer came to her.

"The initials at the base of the statue! Let me think—what were they?"

"N. R.," Jean announced triumphantly.

"Nina Regan!" Louise exclaimed. "Oh, but it's so unlikely."

"I don't see why it is," Jean said, defending her assumption. "Nina Regan was confined at Pinecrest, and for all we know she may have made the statue."

"Possibly Mrs. Grantland would recall the name if she were to hear it," Evelyn suggested.

"That's what I thought," Jean agreed enthusiastically. "Let's hurry over to her house right now and ask her if Nina Regan fashioned that figure."

Louise added in a hushed voice, "Perhaps we could apprehend the runaway ourselves for the authorities."

CHAPTER III

LETTIE'S TRICKERY

MRS. GRANTLAND was surprised at seeing the three girls again so soon after their recent visit.

"Would you remember the name of the person who sculptured 'The Recluse' if you were to hear it again?" Jean demanded breathlessly.

"Why, I'm not certain," the woman said doubtfully.

"Was it Nina Regan?" Louise questioned hopefully.

"I remember now that the first name was Nina! Yes, I do believe that's it."

The girls accordingly related their experience at the police station. Mrs. Grantland was highly indignant at Warden Norton's accusations.

"I hope Aunt Harriet doesn't hear them before we have a chance to explain," Louise smiled.

"She'd be very upset," Jean chuckled.

The girls asked permission to look again at the little statue which had intrigued their

17

interest. Mrs. Grantland accompanied them to the salon.

"Dear me, if I had known that Nina Regan had such a black record I might not have bought the piece." She laughed ruefully. "Yet, I guess I should have succumbed to it anyway. I couldn't have resisted such a beautiful piece of work."

"Did you buy the statue from the prison authorities?" Louise asked.

"No, it came indirectly through a friend. It seems to me she said she had purchased it from a peddler."

"Nina Regan escaped from the reformatory many months ago," Louise commented. "I wonder—" She broke off in an exclamation of startled surprise.

The others turned to see what had frightened her. Ex-Warden Norton was standing in the doorway which opened out into the garden! He had trespassed upon the grounds. Then, seeing the girls through the glass door, he had deliberately opened it and stepped into the salon.

"Mr. Norton!" Jean exclaimed, terrified by the tense expression on his face.

Mrs. Grantland thrust herself between the man and the girls.

"What do you mean by entering my house without permission?" she said severely.

Not in the least abashed, the intruder pointed a long, thin finger at Louise.

"I traced that girl to your home, ma'am. Her name is Nina Regan, and even if the police are stupid, she can't fool me! She's a dangerous character, ma'am."

"You are greatly mistaken," Mrs. Grantland retorted impatiently. "These girls are all well known to me. I must ask you to leave at once."

The man appeared not to hear her. He had noticed the little figure which Louise was holding, and his eyes gleamed.

"There's my proof!" he shouted triumphantly. "Nina Regan made that statue when she was at the reformatory. She came here today to get it!"

Although the ex-warden's accusation definitely established the fact that Nina Regan had fashioned "The Recluse," Louise was too much annoyed at the moment to be as pleased at the information as she might otherwise have been. She had visions of another visit to the police station.

"You have made a ridiculous mistake!" Mrs. Grantland said sharply, summoning a servant. "I bought that statue from a friend, and while I do not deny that it may have been the work of Nina Regan, I do know that she is not in this room now."

"If that girl isn't Nina Regan, then she's

her double!" exclaimed the obnoxious Norton.

"We'll not discuss it," Mrs. Grantland said coldly. "Really, Mr. Norton, I must ask you to leave."

The man was on the point of refusing, but changed his mind as Mrs. Grantland's houseman suddenly appeared at the door.

"All right, I'll go," he grumbled, "but I still think that girl is either Nina Regan or some relative of hers." He squinted again at Louise as he shuffled toward the door which the servant significantly held open. "You're not her sister, are you?"

"No, I'm not," Louise snapped.

At the door Norton paused again, then stumbled outside, mumbling to himself. Jean could distinctly catch the words, "I'll get Nina Regan *yet!*"

"Lock all the doors," Mrs. Grantland directed the servant. "Then see that Mr. Norton is kept off the grounds. I don't trust him."

"He seems slightly demented," Louise declared.

Jean glanced at the wall clock. The hour was growing late. She said that they would have to hurry back to Starhurst, or else miss dinner.

"You're not going alone," Mrs. Grantland said emphatically. "I shall take you in my automobile."

Despite the girls' protests she insisted upon accompanying them personally.

"I don't believe Mr. Norton will dare to bother us again," Evelyn ventured.

"I'm not so sure of that," Mrs. Grantland returned with a troubled frown. "He seems to be a peculiar character. You girls should be very cautious."

"We surely will, Mrs. Grantland," replied Louise.

The gong for dinner had just sounded when the girls reached Starhurst. They hurriedly thanked their friend for her kindness and dashed off to the dining room, little thinking that Mrs. Grantland intended to consult with Mr. and Mrs. Crandall, under whose efficient direction the school was operated.

The caller remained with the professor and his wife for nearly half an hour. When she left she felt assured that Jean and Louise would be carefully guarded, for the Crandalls had promised her that the school watchman would be told to use the utmost caution in keeping strangers off the property.

Jean and Louise entered the dining hall five minutes late. As they seated themselves at the table, Lettie cast a malicious glance in their direction. The Dana girls had expected her to play the part of a tattler, and she did.

"Late again," Lettie said with acid sweetness. "But this time I suppose you couldn't help it—since you were detained at the police station."

She spoke in unnecessarily loud tones, so that students at nearby tables looked curiously at the Danas, and Ina Mason giggled.

Louise had intended to relate what had happened at Penfield, but impulsively decided to tell nothing. She accordingly smiled disarmingly.

"Why, yes, Lettie, you seem to know all about it. By the way, did you finish the book you were reading? 'Prison Walls,' wasn't it?"

Lettie shot a worried glance at Miss Aiken, her teacher of Literature, who disapproved of all trashy volumes of fiction, and mumbled an inaudible reply. When it came to a battle of words, she had never been a match for either of the Dana girls. It angered her that they were able to dismiss the incident so carelessly. Why had they been taken to the police station? If only she could find out!

Unwittingly, Mrs. Crandall brought to her the information she sought. As the girls were leaving the dining hall, the headmistress spoke to Louise at the door, and Lettie lingered to listen.

"Mrs. Grantland told me about that dreadful man who caused you so much trouble at the police station, my dear. I have warned the watchman to use exceptional caution, but you must be on your guard.''

"I will,'' Louise promised. "One encounter with Warden Norton has convinced me that he has some sort of an obsession about this Nina Regan, whom he claims I resemble.''

Jean nudged her sister warningly, but it was too late. Lettie had already heard enough to arouse her curiosity. She could almost guess what had transpired at the police station. She moved on, feeling very well pleased with herself.

Several other students had overheard the conversation, and presently Louise and Jean were forced to tell the entire story. They found themselves looked upon as heroines, especially so when the watchman in his regular rounds would pass beneath their studio window time and again.

It was inevitable that Lettie should eventually learn all the details of the encounter with Norton. Inspired by the information, she sought her toady, Ina Mason.

"Ina, didn't you tell me you saw a picture of Warden Norton in the morning paper?''

"Yes, I did.''

"Try to get me a copy. We'll play a good joke on that smart aleck Louise!''

Lettie's "joke" required an evening's preparation. With the picture of Ex-Warden Norton before her as a guide, she spent hours at her dressing table experimenting with grease paint. Meanwhile, Ina Mason ransacked the building in an effort to locate a suit of men's clothes. She finally obtained one from the gardener. At midnight, behind locked doors, Lettie tried on the masculine attire, and regarded herself proudly in the mirror.

"How do I look, Ina?" she asked.

"Just like the picture of that man Norton, Lettie. My! I can see Louise's face when you jump at her in that disguise! It will give her a fearful scare."

Lettie frowned. She removed the heavy glasses and make-up, and locked her costume in a lower bureau drawer.

"What puzzles me now is how I'll ever get a chance to use these things, Ina," she said.

"You'll have to be careful."

"Yes," said Lettie with a worried look, "if I get caught I might be expelled."

"You'll find a way," Ina said confidently.

The opportunity came the following afternoon. The sophomore class in geology had on its schedule that day a hike to an old stone quarry near by. Louise had assumed that she was to go with the rest, and therefore was disappointed when Mrs. Crandall suggested that it might be safer for her to remain at the school.

"But the hike is supervised," Louise protested. "With a teacher along, surely nothing could happen to me."

"Does the excursion mean a great deal to you?"

"Yes, it does, Mrs. Crandall. I've never visited the quarry. We're to inspect the various rock layers and search for pre-historic relics."

"Then you may go with the others," Mrs. Crandall consented. "After all, I doubt if Warden Norton would dare to trouble you again."

Elated, Louise ran off to don her hiking clothes. After looking through her wardrobe she decided that it would be too much effort to put on slacks, so substituted a thick woolen skirt and heavy hiking boots.

About twenty other girls, including Doris Harland, Nell Carson and Margaret Glenn, were assembled in the courtyard when Louise and Jean joined the group. The geology instructor checked up on the students.

"Is everyone here?" she asked. "Where is Lettie Briggs?"

"She has a headache and isn't coming," Ina informed the teacher, avoiding the woman's eyes.

"This is the second time she has failed to join a field excursion," the instructor said. "I shall have to report her to Mrs. Crandall **as** being absent.''

The Dana girls and their friends were secretly pleased that Lettie had remained at the school. As a rule Ina would go nowhere without her chum and it struck Louise as singular that this particular hike should prove to be an exception.

"Ina seems to be excited about something," Jean presently commented to her sister as they tramped side by side along a forest trail.

"Yes, she's pretty nervous," Louise agreed. "It wouldn't surprise me if Lettie were up to some kind of a trick, and Ina knows about it."

En route to the stone quarry the group halted occasionally as the instructor called attention to interesting rock formations along the path. It was noticeable that Ina took no notes and paid scant attention to what was being said.

The students ate their sandwiches at the quarry, and warmed cocoa over a little fire which they built among the rocks. Then they searched for fossils until it was time for them to start back to the school.

Geology had always been one of Louise's favorite subjects, and the brief excursion was not half long enough to satisfy her. As she approached a waterfall where the teacher had paused earlier in the day to give an explanatory lecture, she lingered to examine an outcropping of limestone along the river's edge.

"Hurry up," called Jean, who was far ahead.

"Coming," Louise shouted.

Nevertheless she remained, hammering at the rock with a flat stone. She became too occupied with what she was doing to notice footsteps behind her. Suddenly a low guttural voice entoned the words:

"I've caught you at last, Nina Regan!"

Lettie Briggs, disguised as the ex-warden, with felt hat pulled low over her eyes, sprang from behind a huge boulder. Taken completely off her guard, Louise struggled to her feet. Involuntarily she took a step backwards, tripped over a vine, and stumbled.

She tried to save herself, but could not do so. Down she went, striking her head a cruel blow against the edge of a sharp rock.

"Ha! I guess that will teach you a thing or two!"

Chuckling wickedly to herself, Lettie vanished into the woods.

CHAPTER IV

A Serious Offense

LETTIE had been in such a hurry to escape
before her identity should be discovered, that
she had made no effort to learn if Louise had
been injured by her fall. She did not know
that the Dana girl had struck her head against
a sharp rock, rendering herself senseless.
Leaving the unconscious form upon the river
bank, she darted through the woods, returning to the school by a devious route.

"I hope Ina has sense enough to do as I
told her," she thought.

Meanwhile, Louise had been missed by her
friends. Jean paused on the trail to look
back.

"Whatever became of that sister of mine?"
she demanded. "I suppose she stopped to
look at another rock."

This was Ina Mason's cue. She announced
glibly:

"Oh, she went on ahead of everyone. Didn't
you see her, Jean?"

"I certainly didn't. Are you sure?"

While Jean had no reason to be suspicious

of Ina, it seemed to her that the girl was un-
duly eager to offer unasked-for information.

"I saw her cutting through the woods ten
minutes ago," Ina maintained. "She must
have been in a hurry to get back to the school
before the rest of us."

"It isn't like Louise to streak off that way
without an explanation," Jean said, looking
troubled. "I think I'll go back a little way
and see if I can find her."

"Don't you believe me?" Ina demanded
harshly.

"I thought possibly you might be mistaken."

"Well, I'm not. You'll find your sister at
the school."

Despite Ina's words, Jean turned and walked
back to the first clearing. Since she was far
from the river bank she could catch no glimpse
of Louise. Convinced that she had done Ina
an injustice in not believing her, she returned
to her friends.

"I guess Ina is right," she admitted readily.
"Louise doubtless went on ahead. But it's
strange that none of us saw her."

"Except Ina," Evelyn Starr commented
thoughtfully.

The girls quickened their steps, for Jean
was eager to make certain that Louise was
safe. When she reached the school she ran
to her own room to find out if her sister had

arrived ahead of her. Louise was not there, and nobody had seen her.

Jean grew thoroughly alarmed. She was convinced now that Ina had lied. Louise had not returned to the school!

"She's lost somewhere in the woods," Jean reasoned. "Oh, I should never have listened to that Mason girl!"

The day had been cloudy and evening came on early. As dusk closed in, a terrible fear gripped Jean's heart. Soon it would be dark!

Before she could make up her mind just what to do, Evelyn Starr darted into the room and closed the door. "You haven't found Louise?" she asked tensely.

"No. I must notify Professor and Mrs. Crandall. I'm afraid my sister is lost!"

"I've just learned something," Evelyn said tersely. "One of the girls saw Lettie Briggs leave the school not ten minutes after our group started off!"

"Which direction did she take?"

"The one toward the woods. She came back a little ahead of the class and disappeared into her room carrying something in a bundle. Do you suppose she could explain Louise's disappearance?"

"Ina did act strangely. It may be you're right. I'm going to place the matter before Mrs. Crandall."

On the way to the office Jean met the Briggs girl in the hall.

"Lettie, have you seen Louise?" she asked anxiously.

"How could I when I've been here all day?"

"But you haven't, Lettie. Someone saw you going into the woods."

"I just went for a little walk. Anyway, what I do is my business."

Jean was desperate, and cried, "Please, Lettie, if you know what has happened to Louise, tell me. I'm very much worried."

The appeal moved the girl for an instant. She seemed on the verge of disclosing something, but changed her mind. With a shrug of her shoulders she moved off.

"She *does* know what has happened to Louise," Jean told herself angrily.

She went to the office and made a clear statement of the case to Professor and Mrs. Crandall, telling them exactly what had occurred and the way Lettie had acted.

"This is indeed serious," Professor Crandall murmured, rubbing his hands together, a habit of his when he was perturbed. "The poor girl may be lost in the forest, and night is coming on. We must do something about it immediately."

"Organize searching parties," Mrs. Crandall said tersely. In an emergency she was always the one to act. "And don't notify the police just yet. Such publicity always harms the reputation of the school."

As she spoke, Mrs. Crandall pressed a call button on her desk. When the summons was answered by an attendant she ordered that Lettie Briggs be sent in at once.

The girl came reluctantly, glancing uneasily from Jean to Mrs. Crandall. She knew why she was wanted, and could not help but disclose it by her guilty expression. But when Mrs. Crandall questioned her regarding her actions she adopted a brazen manner.

"Yes, it's true I went into the woods for a walk," she confessed, "but I didn't have a bundle of any kind with me."

"Did you see Louise?"

Lettie hesitated. By this time she, too, had begun to wonder why the elder Dana had failed to return. She felt a little sick as she recalled that the girl had fallen upon the rocks. Perhaps it would be well to give Mrs. Crandall a clue as to what had happened.

"I did see her," she admitted. "I recall she was standing near the waterfall. She was hammering at some rocks."

Once more the headmistress pressed a button. She did not address Lettie further until she had given complete instructions to the searching party which was just leaving Starhurst. Jean, convinced that she had a clue as to where Louise could be found, hurried off to join Professor Crandall, who was leading the search.

"Lettie, I believe you know more about this affair than you will admit," the principal said severely. "Your actions today were suspicious, to say the least. Go to your room and remain there until you are called!"

While Jean and her friends were hurrying to the river, Louise still lay where she had fallen upon the rock, too stunned to move. It was a long time before full consciousness returned to her.

"I wonder what happened?" she muttered to herself, trying to sit up. Her head felt as if it would split, and a huge bump stood out upon her forehead.

"Now I remember," she thought, as she staggered to her feet. "Warden Norton sprang at me from behind a boulder. After that everything went black."

Things were threatening to turn black again, she discovered. She found herself weak and sick. To save herself from falling she clutched at a willow sapling. As she sagged against the slender trunk, it bent under her weight. She was too stunned to recover her balance and fell headlong into the swift-moving stream.

Louise was a skillful swimmer, but was in

no condition to battle such a strong current. After several vain attempts to do so, she turned on her back and floated along, content to keep her head above water. Not until the river narrowed and she was able to push herself into a shallow place did she succeed in reaching one bank.

She dragged herself out, and for several minutes lay flat upon the sandy shore. At length some strength returned to her, and she arose. As she looked about her, she realized she was in unfamiliar territory amid a growth of dense, tall trees. The river had carried her a long way from the waterfall.

Louise knew that the safest method of reaching her friends would be by following the bank of the stream to the place where she had met disaster. Her sister and the other students doubtless would look for her there. Yet there was no path along the edge, and furthermore she wanted to avoid meeting Warden Norton again. After a slight hesitation she started off through the woods.

The bedraggled girl did not have the remotest suspicion that her present condition was the result of one of Lettie's tricks. Darkness came on rapidly, and before long Louise began to regret that she had not decided to follow the stream.

"I believe I'll go back before it's too late,"

she decided. "If I'm not careful I'll lose my way entirely."

She retraced her steps but failed to find the river. Her dress had not completely dried, and she shivered from the cold. Louise realized now that she was hopelessly lost. She walked along aimlessly with little opportunity of stumbling upon the right trail. To keep up her courage she began to whistle, but this brought her only scant comfort.

"I can't go on much longer," she said to herself. "I'm just about exhausted."

Louise staggered on a few more yards, then halted. A familiar sound came to her ears. It was the roar of an automobile motor.

"I've found a road at last!" she gasped in relief.

Plunging through the entangling vines and weeds, the weary girl came presently to a barbed-wire fence that marked the end of the timber tract. As she crawled under the wires, an automobile with blinding headlights whizzed by her on the road.

"I'll soon be back at Starhurst now," she thought. "Some kind woman will give me a lift."

Hitch-hiking was a new experience to Louise. In vain did she signal to the driver of an approaching car. It slowed down, only to speed on again.

"I guess my appearance goes against me," she reflected ruefully. "I am indeed a sorry sight."

Two more cars went by without stopping. Louise was growing discouraged when a sedan with an out-of-state license came to a halt by the side of the road in response to her hopeful signal.

"Where are you going?" a woman's voice called out before the Dana girl could speak.

"Starhurst," Louise cried eagerly.

"Jump in, then," said the man driver, flinging open the door of the back seat.

Louise would have liked to have explained the reason for her unkempt appearance, but the couple did not seem to be especially interested. The woman scarcely looked at the girl after the first glance. She studied a road map and her husband attended strictly to his driving. The two were taking a long cross country tour, and were intent only upon making good time.

Louise was weary and drowsy, and closed her eyes for an instant. The next thing she knew, someone was shaking her by the arm.

"Wake up," the driver's wife was saying.

"Are we there?" Louise mumbled.

"Where was it you wanted to go?" the woman asked a trifle impatiently. "Did you say Starhurst?"

By this time Louise was thoroughly awake.

"Yes, to the Starhurst School for Girls. It's near Penfield."

"But we thought you meant a town by the name of Starhurst!"

"Where am I now?" Louise gasped. "Is Penfield far from here?"

"It's about forty miles back," the driver told her. "And the unfortunate part of it is that we'll have to put you off here!"

CHAPTER V

STRANDED

LOUISE was stunned by this information. Forty miles from Penfield! Her friends and Jean must be frantic with worry over her absence.

"I wish we could take you back," the driver said regretfully. "We'd do it, only we're in a hurry."

"You probably can catch a ride without much trouble," the woman added.

There was nothing Louise could do but thank the couple and get out of the car at the next crossroad. Sick at heart, she watched her late acquaintances disappear beyond the bend.

"Now what am I to do?" she thought. "Here I am, stranded."

It was long past dinner-time, and Louise was hungry. Her head was aching from the blow she had received from her fall, and she felt weak and tired as she surveyed her surroundings.

She glimpsed a filling station across the way, and took heart. She would make a telephone call to the school and explain her predicament. Hopefully she searched her pockets for a coin. She did not have even a nickel. She had removed everything from her clothes before starting on the hike!

Louise wandered aimlessly toward the filling station. A car drove in, and an attendant came out to operate one of the pumps. Louise eyed him speculatively.

"I might ask him for a loan," she thought. "Still, he doesn't look very approachable, although one cannot always judge character by a face."

She waited until the auto had driven away, then walked over to the man in uniform. His look as he regarded her wrinkled, muddy clothing, the bedraggled condition of her hair, and the smudges of dirt upon her face made Louise very self-conscious.

"Pardon me," she murmured nervously, "but would you lend me some money to telephone?"

"No, I wouldn't lend you a nickel," the man retorted, moving toward the office. "And don't let me catch you loitering around here."

Humiliated, Louise hurried away.

"He treated me as if I were an ordinary beggar," she thought bitterly.

Suddenly she caught a reflection of herself in the plate glass window of a restaurant which adjoined the office of the filling station. For the first time she realized that her appearance was not in her favor.

"I look as if I had been hitch-hiking for at least a month," she acknowledged ruefully. "Perhaps he thought I was the escaped Nina Regan."

From an open window of the place the delightful aroma of roasting meat was wafted to her, and it made her fairly faint with longing. For fully five minutes she stood watching a golden brown chicken which was slowly crisping on a barbecue.

"I'm going to ask the man who runs this place if he will help me," she decided.

The proprietor had seen her accost the filling station attendant. Before she could tell him her story, he said sharply:

"Sorry, you can't come in here. I've nothing for you."

Louise retreated, preferring to starve rather than be humbled further. She decided that the motorists might be more kindly. If she were to start walking on toward Penfield someone might offer her a ride.

Slowly she made her way along the side of the pavement. Cars whizzed by so rapidly that she felt the cold wind swish past her cheek. No one stopped, or even took the slightest notice of her signalling.

When Louise had abandoned all hope, a sedan slackened its pace. She ran over to the car, elated that at last someone had taken pity upon her.

"Want a ride?" a gruff voice asked.

Louise stiffened. She recognized the tones. They could belong only to Ex-Warden Norton! With a stifled cry of alarm she backed away, but a spotlight was turned full upon her face.

"So it's you, Nina Regan!" the man cried. "Now I know you're going to take a ride with me."

He sprang from the car. Louise darted from him but was too weary and weak to run far. The warden overtook her, and grasped her roughly by the wrist.

"Into the car!" he ordered tersely. "You're going back to jail."

Louise began to sob. After her many bitter experiences of the day, this was indeed the last straw. She was afraid of Harold Norton, believing him to be somewhat demented.

"Why can't you leave me alone?" she cried. "First you jump out of the bushes at me, and when I am knocked unconscious, you leave me lying on the river bank. Then you follow me and again make your ridiculous charge that I am Nina Regan."

The ex-warden looked bewildered. He did not comprehend the trend of her statement.

He only knew that by some lucky chance she had played into his hands, and he intended to drive her to Pinecrest Reformatory without a second's delay.

"Now don't try any tricks or I'll put those hands of yours in steel cuffs," he warned. "And if you make a move to jump from the car, I'll tie you up!"

Louise did not doubt but that he would, for he had a wild look in his eyes. He drove like a maniac, crossing the road from side to side, so that the car swayed dangerously. The girl's eyes riveted themselves upon the speedometer, and she clung to the seat, expecting each moment to be her last.

Trees, telephone poles and fences whizzed by the fenders. Warden Norton's foot remained pressed hard upon the gasoline pedal, not even letting up at the approach of another car. Blinded by the bright lights, he would swerve perilously toward the center of the road.

"You'll kill us both!" Louise screamed. "Slow down!"

The man paid no attention to her. They swung around a curve, barely missing the ditch, and Louise was hurled with great force against the window glass. A mile farther on they avoided striking another large car by a hair's-breadth.

"Are you blind?" Louise cried fearfully. "If you don't slow down——"

The warning ended in a scream. At last Norton had lost control of the car. Too late he tried to stop. The front wheels went off the road and began to wobble. The automobile staggered like a crazy thing, and then turned over in a ditch.

Louise was badly shaken and somewhat stunned by the crash, but fortunately was not hurt. With difficulty she pushed open the door of the machine and climbed out.

She was free!

A low moan from beneath the wreckage drew her attention to Norton, who was pinned behind the steering wheel.

"What shall I do?" she murmured.

Now was her chance to escape. If she were to aid the man, he might again turn upon her. But even as the thought occurred to her, Louise bent down to help the stricken driver. She tugged at the wreckage which held him a prisoner.

The ex-warden's eyes were closed and she believed that he had been badly injured. As she succeeded in freeing his limbs, he aroused himself.

"You tried to kill me!" he muttered. "You threw us into the ditch by jerking my arm!"

Louise was dumbfounded at such an accusation. It was unbelievable, but the ex-warden actually did think that she had tried to wreck the car. He would doubtless testify to that effect. Such was the reward for her mercy!

Norton sat up. He was not seriously injured, and in another minute or two would have completely recovered his strength.

Louise took to her heels. Scrambling under a wire fence, she ran blindly through the dark woods, with no idea where she was. She stumbled over vines and fallen logs, still keeping on. She was out of breath by the time she reached a small clearing.

Imagining that she heard footsteps behind her, she ran doggedly on. Directly in her path lay an open, abandoned well. It was too dark for her to see the yawning gap in the earth.

Not until it was too late for her to save herself did she have the slightest warning of her fate. Her feet plunged through the floor of vines which screened the hole, and with a sickening sensation she felt herself falling through inky space.

CHAPTER VI

At the Hermitage

LOUISE struck the bottom of the well with a splash and a thud. Rocks, sticks, and loose pieces of cement came hurtling down upon her head.

She struggled to her feet, bruised but unhurt. The water came only to her knees, but the smooth walls of the well were higher than her head. She was trapped!

"Such a place in which to die," she told herself grimly. "No one will think of looking for me here in this forsaken place—miles from Penfield, and in a well!"

Her courage, which had held out admirably until now, gave way. Although she knew it would do her no good, she shouted for help at the top of her lungs. Her wavering voice echoed strangely, mockingly.

Louise could not sit down except in water. Never before in all her life had she experienced such a hopeless feeling. She visioned herself collapsing miserably upon the bottom of the well, and drowning.

She shouted again for help. Was it her

imagination, or did she hear someone approaching? She did not dare hope. Suddenly a voice called out through the night.

"Where are you?"

"In the well!" Louise shouted frantically.

There was a long wait; then a face peered down at her. The light from a lantern shone full upon her, illuminating the damp walls.

"I'll have you out in a minute!" an old man called down. "Keep up your courage!"

The face disappeared. Louise spent ten miserable, but hopeful minutes. Then the man reappeared with a rope which he lowered into the well. Louise grasped it, and was pulled to safety.

She was so exhausted, having suffered such a shock by her recent ordeal, that she scarcely glanced at her rescuer. Later she vaguely recalled that he was a frail man who wore loose-fitting garments which completely enveloped his figure, and that his long hair blew in clouds about his face. At any other time she might have been frightened by the wild appearance of this person who obviously was a hermit. Now she leaned heavily against him, feeling that she had found a friend.

"Who are you?" the rescuer asked in a high-pitched voice as he supported her. "How did you get here?" Before she could answer, he added, "Never mind. You are in trouble. I will give you food and shelter for the night."

"You are very kind," Louise murmured, and then fainted.

When she opened her eyes the Dana girl found herself in a rocky retreat. Her gaze roved slowly about the walls, which were dimly illuminated by two sputtering candles on a battered table. The room seemed damp. Louise felt certain that she was in an underground cave, until she saw a window through which the stars were visible.

"It must be a hermitage," she said to herself. "A cave room built into a rocky ledge."

"Do you feel any better now?" asked a voice suddenly.

Turning her head slightly, Louise saw the hermit bending over her. She would have been terrified had not his eyes assured her that he was kind. The man held a bowl of steaming soup in his hands, and urged Louise to drink it.

The girl downed it in great gulps.

"Half-starved," the hermit murmured. He went for more.

Louise smiled slightly at the words. After all, she had missed only one meal; yet within the past few hours it seemed to her that she had endured a lifetime of suffering.

The hermit brought bread, apples and fresh milk. Louise's strength began to return after she had eaten, and she ventured a question.

"Can you tell me how far I am from Penfield?"

"A long, long way."

Louise remained silent a moment. Then she said, "You haven't told me your name."

"My name—" echoed the hermit. "Why, no, I—" He hastily arose, picked up the empty soup bowl, and disappeared through the door.

"I shouldn't have asked him that," Louise ruminated. "I suppose he has a very good reason for being a recluse and keeping his identity to himself."

She stretched herself again upon the couch. For the moment she was too weary to think. Her eyes closed, but she did not sleep.

Presently she became aware that the door was ajar. Some distance away, dimly visible, there stood a white figure. Was it motioning for her to leave the place?

Louise sat up, her nerves on edge. Was this a human being, or could it merely be the product of her imagination? Perhaps someone was trying to warn her.

The hermit returned at that moment, and closed the door behind him. He noticed the pallor of Louise's face.

"You're not feeling worse?" he queried anxiously.

"I think I had better go," Louise said nervously. "I don't like to trouble you."

"You can't leave tonight. You would lose your way in the woods. In the morning, perhaps, after you have rested."

So saying, he went out again. All was silent for a time; so still it was, that Louise could hear her heart pounding.

Suddenly she became aware of another sound —a steady rat-a-tat-tat, with irregularly spaced dots and dashes. Where it was coming from, or what made the strange sounds, she could not guess.

She concluded that it was a code of some sort; yet she could make nothing out of it. The conviction grew upon her that she had stumbled into some sort of a hide-out. Perhaps the hermit was flashing word of her arrival.

"I'm leaving this place," Louise said to herself determinedly. Under these circumstances she did not crave adventure or excitement.

She sprang up from the couch and moved toward the door. Before she could reach it, however, the hermit entered. Had he been watching her all the time? Louise had no way of finding out.

"I must return to Starhurst tonight," she told him desperately. "Everyone will worry about me. Thank you so much for your kindness."

The hermit swung open the outside door.

Louise was mistaken in thinking that he intended her to leave, however. Instead, he indicated several black clouds which were beginning to blot out the stars.

"There will be a storm soon," he cautioned. "A bad one, I fear."

He closed the door again and Louise offered no further protest. She realized that it would be unwise for her to attempt to reach Starhurst that night. If she had only some way of letting Jean know that she was safe!

The hermit began making up a bed on the couch. He was as efficient as any woman, Louise noted, when he placed clean, though coarse, sheets smoothly over the mattress.

"I shall be in the next room," he said. "If you feel frightened, call me."

He went out, closing the door as he did so. Louise then heard a bolt snap. She saw that the outside exit remained unlocked, and a feeling of relief came over her.

The Dana girl did not intend to sleep. Yet, after blowing out the candles, she felt a drowsy warmth creep over her, and soon she dozed off. The night was half gone, when she awoke to find that it was raining. Great drops pelted against the window panes. Vivid flashes of lightning illuminated the room.

Louise arose and looked out. She opened the door for an instant, and as she did so a gust of wind drove a sheet of water against her.

She was about to go back to bed, satisfied that she had made no mistake in deciding to remain at the hermitage, when a weird cry echoed through the cavern-like room. This was followed by a man's high-pitched laughter.

Louise crouched against the wall, listening intently, but the sounds were not repeated.

"Oh, why, why did I agree to stay here?" Louise asked herself. "I'll be a nervous wreck long before morning."

Sleep was out of the question, so she lit one of the candles, wrapped herself in a blanket, and decided to sit up the rest of the night. The hours dragged slowly by.

Louise meanwhile grew more and more courageous. She had noticed earlier that two inside doors branched off from the room which she occupied. One of them was locked, she knew, but she decided to try the other. She tiptoed over to it, and softly turned the knob. The hinges creaked slightly as the door opened.

At first it was too dark for Louise to see the interior of the room, and she did not wish to use the candle. As her eyes grew more and more accustomed to the darkness, she noticed a strange object in the far corner of the chamber. It was a cradle.

After a brief hesitation she walked stealthily

over to it. A little child was sleeping soundly upon a pillow.

"Of all things!" Louise exclaimed softly. "This is surely the house of miracles and mystery!"

The youngster had kicked off one of its blankets, and Louise bent down to straighten the covers. As she did so, she noticed that the little one was crippled.

"Oh, how dreadful," the girl thought. "I wonder if this poor child belongs to the hermit."

She straightened the blankets and stole back to her own room, so upset by what she had seen that for the remainder of the night she sat up, tense and watchful. As the first rays of the rising sun appeared in the east, Louise breathed more freely.

"I must escape before the hermit awakens," she decided.

As she stole out, she paused for a moment to look back at the vine-clad walls, feeling certain that the hermitage guarded some deep, stirring mystery.

"Some day I'm coming back to find out what it is," she said to herself. "And I can thank the strange old man for his kindness at that time."

Louise did not know where she was, nor how to reach the nearest town. The early morning air was cold, and the light sweater she wore was hardly sufficient protection. Her clothes were dry, however, so she was more comfortable than she had been the day before.

For an hour Louise trudged through the woods. After what seemed to her an eternity there came the far-away whistle of a locomotive, so she headed in the direction from which the sound came. Shortly thereafter her path led her to some tracks.

"I'll follow the rails until I reach a town," she decided.

On and on she walked, counting railroad ties until she lost interest. Her feet hurt her. She wished for nothing more in all the world than a good hot breakfast of eggs and buttered toast.

At last she approached a trestle, underneath which several small boys were fishing in a tiny creek. They looked at her with interest, but kept watch of the bobbing corks.

"Boys, can you tell me the way to the nearest town?" she asked.

"Sure," a freckle-faced lad in overalls answered with a friendly grin. "You mean Clairtown."

"Yes," Louise agreed instantly. Any name would have satisfied her.

"It's only a quarter of a mile, and the quickest way to get there is to keep on walking."

The prospect of trudging even a quarter of a mile farther was repellent to Louise at the moment, so she climbed down beside the boys and sat on the ground to rest.

"Are you a lady tramp?" one of the lads asked.

Louise laughed. She told them something of her predicament, carefully avoiding the subject of the hermit.

"Gee, you've sure had an awful time," said a freckle-faced boy with honest sympathy. "I'll bet you're hungry, too."

"Starving. And I haven't a cent with me."

The boys withdrew to the other side of the trestle. After a whispered consultation, they returned. One held out a grimy hand. In his palm rested two dimes.

"Here," he said generously. "Take this, and get yourself something to eat."

Louise was deeply grateful. She knew that to each boy the giving of the money represented the sacrifice of a candy bar or an ice cream cone. Yet those twenty cents meant much to her. She could now telephone to Starhurst.

"I'll see that you get your money back several times over," she promised the boys. "Let me have your names and addresses."

The lads wrote them on a scrap of paper for her. Then wearily Louise trudged onward.

Rounding a curve, she came within view of Clairtown. She stopped at the first eating place and asked to use the telephone. A connection was made with the Starhurst School, and Mrs. Crandall's harassed voice reached her ear.

"Louise! Louise Dana! Is it really you?"

"Yes, I'm at a place called Clairtown, at the Elite Restaurant."

"We've been searching everywhere for you. Your sister is almost frantic. Are you sure you are all right?"

Louise began a hurried account of her adventures, only to be warned by the operator that her time was up. She had no more money and it did not occur to her to ask that the charges be reversed. She hung up the receiver with the happy assurance that her friends would come for her as soon as they could make the long drive.

The little restaurant was warm and pleasant. From the kitchen floated the tantalizing aroma of ham frying.

"If I only had some money—" Louise thought.

She noticed that the waitress was watching her curiously. She was of about the same size and build as Louise, and this gave her an idea. She walked over to the counter.

"Would you consider exchanging a plate of

ham and eggs for a good Angora wool sweater, slightly soiled?"

"Is that the sweater you have on?" The girl looked it over appraisingly.

"Yes," Louise replied.

"O.K. Hand it over. Order whatever you want for breakfast and I'll stand the bill."

"I'll have a plate of ham and eggs," said Louise, her eyes glowing. "Lots of buttered toast. A glass of orange juice, a few wheat cakes, and——"

"Huh, I guess you *are* hungry." Then upon closer scrutiny, "You look like the picture I saw in the newspaper of Nina Regan who escaped from the reformatory."

Louise looked startled. "You're wrong," she stammered, but the waitress had fled. Was she going to fill her order, or call the police?

CHAPTER VII

SAFE AT SCHOOL

AT Starhurst School for Girls everyone rejoiced over the fact that Louise Dana had been found unharmed. Throughout the night searching parties had combed the woods in an attempt to locate her. Their alarm had increased when Jean had found her sister's initialed handkerchief by the bank of the stream near the place where she had fallen in.

The river had been dragged. Frantic with worry, Jean had remained at the scene until dawn. She had postponed breaking the news to her Aunt Harriet, thinking that at any hour her sister might be found. But she was on her way to telephone to Oak Falls when Louise's welcome message reached the school.

"Oh, how thankful I am," Jean declared, half laughing, half crying. "We must go to her at once," she said to Mrs. Crandall.

"Certainly. I've already ordered a car."

The night had been a trying ordeal for everyone. Even the headmistress, who prided herself upon being able to meet any emergency calmly, looked haggard and worn.

"Tell me, has she been found?" Lettie Briggs asked Jean, as she was on her way upstairs to get wraps for both herself and Louise.

"Yes, she's at Clairtown. How she ever got there we don't know."

"At Clairtown! But when I saw her—" Lettie broke off in confusion.

"What was that?"

"Nothing. I was just going to say I didn't see how she happened to be there."

Lettie hastily retreated.

"That girl had plenty to do with it," Jean told herself grimly. "There's something queer about the way she acts."

At Clairtown Louise was waiting in the little restaurant where she had eaten her breakfast. The waitress had decided she was not Nina Regan. As the automobile bearing Mr. and Mrs. Crandall and Jean drove up, she dashed out to meet them.

Jean hugged her sister convulsively.

"Oh, I'm so glad to see you. What happened? You're a sight! Your stockings and dress are torn! And whatever became of your lovely sweater?"

"I ate it up," Louise laughed, and hurriedly explained how she had bought some food.

She was shivering from the cold. Mrs. Crandall wrapped a heavy coat about the girl, as she settled herself in the soft cushions of the car. During the drive back Louise related her experiences. Now that she was far away from the hermitage, the things which had occurred there seemed almost like a dream. Although Mrs. Crandall listened to her tale with an absorbing interest, it was clear she thought the girl had imagined some of the more harrowing events.

"My dear, after falling into a river and a well, I don't wonder that you became nervous, I know I should have seen all sorts of strange things myself."

"But I actually did see them, Mrs. Crandall. I'm sure I didn't imagine them."

"Of course not," the woman said kindly. "I think that after such an experience you should be in bed. A complete rest with absolute quiet is what you need."

After a little while Mrs. Crandall mentioned Lettie Briggs.

"I am very happy to learn that she had nothing to do with your unfortunate accident, Louise. I fear I was unjustly suspicious of the girl."

"She was seen returning to the school from the woods with a bundle of clothing under her arm," Jean told her sister. "Of course, if it was Warden Norton who frightened you, Lettie could have had nothing to do with it."

"It must have been Warden Norton," Louise said. "Naturally I was so startled at the time that I scarcely glanced at his face. But I could see him plainly enough when he sped off with me in his car."

Despite her sister's story, Jean was not entirely convinced that Lettie was blameless. She still felt that in some way the Briggs girl had been responsible for Louise's unfortunate experience.

Her interest had been aroused also concerning the hermit and the quaint cave-like place in which he dwelt. As soon as she was alone with her sister, she asked for additional details.

"There's a deep mystery connected with the place," Louise declared. "If I hadn't been so fearful, I would have stayed and found out what it was."

"You did the right thing by leaving. One must use judgment together with courage. But there's nothing to prevent our going there sometime—together."

"Sometime," Louise murmured. Then, dropping back against her pillow, she fell into a deep sleep.

Jean was eager to visit the hermitage. She decided not to mention her desire, however, until Louise should have fully recovered from her harrowing experience.

News of the older Dana girl's return had swept the school. The story of her adventures were told and retold, distorted slightly and glorified exceedingly. Louise found herself to be a heroine in the eyes of the students. Whenever she would leave her room a host of friends would gather about her.

The attention showered upon Lettie's rival annoyed the Briggs girl exceedingly. In order to get into the limelight, she began to talk of a fine birthday present she was to receive from her parents.

"I am to have a diamond ring," she announced. "Not a cheap one, either. My father is buying the biggest stone he can find."

Lettie spoke of the ring so often to her classmates, that they grew bored with it, and at the mention of diamonds would begin to yawn.

"Let's play a joke on her," Jean proposed to several of the girls who had gathered in the Dana rooms. "We could spring it the night before her birthday!"

"Does it have anything to do with diamonds?" Louise laughed.

"It does. Do you want to hear the details?"

They all did. Amid a great deal of merriment the little group laid their plans, and then someone, looking from a window, announced the coming of the postman.

Mail-time at Starhurst was always an important hour. Long before the arrival of the carrier students would begin to gather in the corridors and eye their letter boxes wistfully.

Louise and Jean were the focal point of attention as they removed a long, bulky envelope bearing their names. The girls deduced at a glance that it came from Uncle Ned Dana, captain of the *Balaska*. He always made a point of sending messages from European ports, and his admiring nieces faithfully saved all kinds of foreign stamps.

"Hurry and open it," Jean urged.

Uncle Ned had written in his usual breezy style, saying he had bought each of his nieces a woolen scarf which they would receive in due course of time. At the very end of the letter a sentence held the Dana girls' attention.

"I will have a passenger sailing with me on the return trip to New York, who says he is looking for a suitable school in which to enroll his young daughter. I told him about Starhurst, and he said he would look it over when he reached the U. S. A.

"If Mr. Harvey Symington should drop in one of these days, you might show him around. Give him your usual sales talk about Starhurst, and I am sure he will be convinced that it is the only worth-while school in America for his daughter Ellen to attend.''

"I think Uncle Ned was poking fun at us in that last sentence,'' Jean twinkled. "But it will be nice meeting his friend. I wonder when Mr. Symington will arrive?''

Almost a week elapsed before the gentleman appeared at the school. As Jean and Louise escorted him from one building to another, they came to learn that their distinguished visitor was a well-known art collector. He had a keen appreciation of the fine Ionic columns which added dignity to the main building, and appeared delighted with the natural beauty of campus and countryside.

"I should like to have my daughter Ellen be a student amid these lovely surroundings,'' he told the girls. "Starhurst is indeed charming.'' He then pointed out a number of effects which the Dana girls had never paid much attention to before—an attractive cornice, a remarkable arched doorway, an unusual stained glass window.

Later the two sisters presented Mr. Symington to Mrs. Crandall, who recognized the name at once, and was pleased that such a distinguished man wished to send a member of his family to the school.

Before leaving he agreed to deliver a brief

lecture upon one of his favorite subjects, that of sculpture. The talk was to be given in the school auditorium, and the students were told they might invite friends not attending the school.

"I wonder if Mrs. Grantland would like to come?" Louise mused. "She's so interested in statuary. It would be nice for her to meet Mr. Symington."

When reached at her home, the good lady assured the Dana girls that she would be delighted to accept. After the lecture, which was by far the most outstanding one of its kind that year at the school, Mrs. Grantland met Mr. Symington and the two began an animated conversation about sculpture.

"Would you like to come to my house and view my private collection?" Mrs. Grantland asked. "I am very proud of my pieces."

The interested man accepted without the slightest hesitation. He seemed pleased when he learned that the Dana girls had been included in the invitation, for he enjoyed their gay conversation. Mrs. Crandall raised no objection to the little excursion, since Mrs. Grantland promised to bring Louise and Jean back before half past ten that night.

Mr. Symington was enthusiastic in his praise of Mrs. Grantland's many fine pieces. When he paused before "The Recluse," he lost his polished restraint, and could not repress his admiration.

"This piece is worth more than any of the others," he declared. "It is a marvelous bit of work—the creation of a true artist."

Later, as Mrs. Grantland was driving Mr. Symington to his hotel and the Dana girls to their school, Jean remarked to Louise that it seemed a great pity that Nina Regan was a fugitive from justice.

"If Mr. Norton has his way about it, she'll be hunted to her dying day," Louise added ruefully. "I wish we could find out whatever became of her—perhaps we could help her."

"I expect to go to Pinecrest Reformatory tomorrow," said Mrs. Grantland to the Dana girls. This society woman had always taken a keen interest in social service work, and during the past few months had devoted much of her time to visiting state institutions. "I am very curious to learn if conditions there have improved since Warden Norton's removal. Yes, I think I'll go tomorrow."

Jean gripped Louise's hand. Her sister understood the signal. She, too, wanted to visit Pinecrest.

"Tomorrow is Saturday," the older girl sighed suggestively. "Such a dull day at Starhurst, too."

"Why don't you two come along with me?

I'd love to have you if you feel sure that it would interest you.''

Jean and Louise fairly hugged each other in anticipation.

"Interest us?" Jean echoed. "I should say it would!''

"Then I'll call for you early—say about nine," Mrs. Grantland smiled, as the car drew up at Starhurst. "Until then—good-bye.''

CHAPTER VIII

AN INTERCEPTED NOTE

"YES, I am Mrs. Selzer," the matron of Pine-crest Reformatory said to the visitors. "You must feel free to look around as much as you like, providing you do not converse with the prisoners. I will conduct you about myself."

She smiled mechanically at Mrs. Grantland, Jean and Louise, who had been ushered into her office. Visitors were looked upon by the busy matron as a necessary annoyance. She closed her desk and locked it with a key which she wore on a ring at her waist. Then she led the way down the long, bleak corridor.

"This is the laundry," she explained, indicating a door to the right. "The girls do all the work for the Reformatory, of course. On the other side of the hall are the kitchens. We'll step inside for a moment."

Sullen-eyed girls in gray uniforms were peeling potatoes, scraping vegetables, and washing dishes. They looked up defiantly as the matron entered with the visitors.

"Each girl must do her share of kitchen work," Mrs. Selzer explained. "However, if

67

we discover that an inmate has a talent for something better—especially creative work, we try to give her an opportunity to express herself. We have several aspiring writers in our group as well as an artist, and at one time we had a talented young woman who sculptured.''

"Not Nina Regan?" Jean asked eagerly.

"Yes, that was her name. I suppose you read about her in the newspapers. She escaped from here some time ago.''

"I have one of her works," Mrs. Grantland remarked. " 'The Recluse.' Possibly you recall it.''

"No, I can't say that I do. But she did a lot of modelling while she was here. I take it that you bought the statue here.''

"Why, no, I didn't. A friend of mine purchased it for me from a street vendor.''

Mrs. Selzer looked surprised.

"That is rather odd. Are you certain the statue was made by Nina Regan?''

"Yes. It bore her initials.''

Mrs. Selzer dropped the subject, and Louise and Jean refrained from bringing it up again. It occurred to them that Nina undoubtedly had been earning her living since her escape by creating and selling statues.

"Nina was an ideal inmate, and it was a shock to me when she ran away," the matron commented. "How often I have thought that

if Warden Norton had treated her more fairly
she might have stayed."

"Was he partial?" Louise questioned.

"Unfortunately, he had favorites. See that
young woman over by the window? Nellie
Brice is her name. She was one of Mr. Norton's favored few. While he was here she
never did a full day's work."

The girls glanced over toward the woman
who had been pointed out to them. She, too,
was garbed in the unbecoming gray costume of
the institution; yet she wore it with an air of
distinction which set her apart from the others.
Her face was vivacious; her black eyes snapped
like brands of fire.

"She looks younger than thirty-two," the
matron said. "Nellie is a widow."

"Why did Norton favor her above the rest?"
Jean asked.

The matron shrugged.

"Why does anyone have likes or dislikes?
He was a strange man, and I make no bones
about saying that we were political enemies.
We never could agree about a thing, especially when it came to the management of
this institution."

"You say he did not like Nina Regan?"
Louise inquired.

"He seemed to dislike her from the very
first. He gave her most of the disagreeable

tasks, and would not permit her to do as much sculpturing as she wanted to. It was disgraceful, the way he pampered Nellie. Yet surprising as it may seem, those two girls were fast friends.''

''Nellie and Nina Regan?'' Mrs. Grantland asked in astonishment.

''Yes. To my knowledge Nellie never made any others here at Pinecrest except Nina.''

''I don't suppose you have a picture of the Regan girl,'' Louise said.

''Why, yes, I have one in my office files. We keep complete records and photos of all inmates who pass through the institution. Wait just a moment, and I'll get it for you.''

She went out the door. No sooner had she disappeared than Nellie Brice sidled over toward the three. She cast a quick glance about the room to see if any of the other inmates were watching her, but they were all busy with their duties at the time.

Nellie spoke to Louise, who was nearest to her.

''Mail this letter for me,'' she whispered. ''And don't let the matron see what you are doing!''

Louise was on the verge of refusing the request, but it was not necessary for her to do so. Mrs. Selzer, returning before she had been expected, had entered the room just as Nellie held out the envelope. The matron darted forward and snatched the missive from the young woman's hand.

"Up to your same old tricks, Nellie Brice! For this, you'll spend a day in solitary confinement!"

Mrs. Selzer examined the envelope which she had seized. Although it was sealed, it had not been addressed.

"Where were you trying to send this letter, Nellie?"

The inmate refused to answer.

"What did she say to you, Miss Dana?" the matron asked Louise.

"She only requested me to mail the letter, Mrs. Selzer. She didn't say where it was to be sent."

"Well, I'll soon find out."

While Nellie looked on angrily, the matron ripped open the envelope and read the contents. The message had been hastily scribbled upon a paper towel, and was addressed to a man named Pat Closky.

"Take good care of the child until I come," the note said. "If plans go through, I'll make the break in two or three days."

After Mrs. Selzer had perused it, she handed the note over to Mrs. Grantland and the Dana girls to read.

"So you were planning to escape, Nellie?"

she questioned severely. "Tell me, who is this man Closky? Where does he live?"

"You'll have to find that out for yourself, Mrs. Selzer."

"You didn't tell me you had a child," the matron said, trying a different method of approach. "If you will answer my questions, I'll forget this offense."

Nellie threw her head back defiantly.

"I'll tell you nothing, Mrs. Selzer. I prefer solitary confinement."

"Very well. You'll get it."

The matron rang a bell for an attendant, and the young woman was led away.

"Just an unfortunate incident," Mrs. Selzer remarked with a sigh. "We have them frequently here."

"It must be difficult to manage so many rebellious girls," Mrs. Grantland commented.

"Yes. But luckily only a few of them cause as much trouble as Nellie." She took a photograph from her pocket and handed it to the Dana girls. "This is Nina Regan."

"Why, she's pretty!" Louise exclaimed. "And she has such a sweet, innocent face."

"Is that all you notice?" Jean asked curiously.

"Why, yes, she has nice features and dark hair——"

"Almost exactly like your own," Jean concluded. "If you were ten or fifteen years older, you'd look like that photo."

"There is a marked resemblance," Mrs. Grantland agreed. "No wonder Mr. Norton thought that you were Nina."

Mrs. Selzer volunteered to conduct the party through the room-cells, but the two Danas were glad that Mrs. Grantland decided against this. They had seen quite enough of Pinecrest Reformatory for one day. The meeting with Nellie Brice, which the matron had termed an "unfortunate incident," had proven especially upsetting to the lady from Penfield.

"It positively makes me ill to think of that young woman being in solitary confinement," she told Jean and Louise as they left the building. "Of course, she broke the rules of the institution and was very impudent. Reformatories must be run strictly. Yet it seems too bad to treat the girl that way."

"Mrs. Selzer appears to be an improvement over Warden Norton, at least," Louise said.

"Yes, I am sure she does the best she can," Mrs. Grantland sighed. "Oh, I almost wish we hadn't come. It was all so depressing."

"Perhaps you'd feel better if we were to have a cup of tea somewhere," Jean suggested.

Her hostess seized upon the idea. "Yes, I think that would strengthen me. Shall we stop at the village?"

On the outskirts of the next town they found a pleasant tea shop, whose quaint decoration appealed to them. The interior was even more interesting, for the owner had spent considerable time and thought in arranging furniture and nick-nacks.

A maid in a white apron escorted the group to a table overlooking the garden. It was just the kind of place to make them forget the depression of that morning. After she had sipped her tea, Mrs. Grantland began chatting in her usual animated fashion.

"Such lovely bric-a-brac," she declared, looking about her. "I love old glassware and china."

The shelf displays in the tea shop were not confined to antiques alone. Louise and Jean were quick to observe an odd-looking piece of statuary that stood upon a nearby pedestal.

As they were about to leave, Jean walked over to examine it more closely. The work portrayed a crippled child being guarded by a watch dog.

"That piece has a workmanship similar to that of 'The Recluse,'" she thought excitedly. "I wonder if Miss Regan could have made this figure, too."

She carefully removed it from the pedestal and examined its base. It bore the familiar initials "N. R."

"Louise," she called, "come here and see what I've found. Another statue by Nina Regan."

"What makes you think so?"

Jean pointed to the initialed base. By this time Mrs. Grantland had sauntered over to them. Her eyes sparkled as she regarded the statue.

"I shall ask the proprietor if she will sell it to me! It would fit so nicely into my collection."

Jean and Louise followed the woman to the front of the shop where the owner was occupied with her accounts.

"Let's try to find out where the statue was purchased," Louise whispered to her sister. "We may discover a clue to Nina Regan's whereabouts."

CHAPTER IX

A Clue

The owner of the tea shop graciously replied to the questions put to her by Mrs. Grantland and the Dana girls.

"I think the statue is interesting, too," she said enthusiastically. "I bought it only a few days ago."

"Where, may I ask?" inquired Louise.

"From a vendor who came through this town. He was an odd character, but if he mentioned his name I have forgotten it."

"Could you describe him?" Jean asked.

"No, I'm afraid I couldn't. He came in just at our busy hour. I was intrigued into buying the statue, for it is unusual."

"You made no mistake," Mrs. Grantland declared. "It is a fine piece, and if you would consider selling it I should like very much to purchase it."

The owner thought over the matter for a moment, then mentioned a price which seemed ridiculously low to Mrs. Grantland. While the proprietor was wrapping up the piece of statuary, Louise suggested that the figures of the child and the dog depicted thereon were realistic enough to have been modeled from true life.

"I think they must have been," the woman agreed. "The vendor mentioned that he had a crippled baby to support. He appeared to be very poor."

En route to Starhurst, Jean and Louise went over the facts they had ferreted out. On the whole, the little group was well satisfied with the day's excursion. Mrs. Grantland felt elated over her purchase. The Dana girls had learned a number of interesting things relating to Nina Regan.

"I just wonder if there might be some connection among Pat Closky, Nellie Brice, and Nina Regan," Louise mused.

"The little statue we discovered today would seem to indicate that there is," Jean agreed. "Nina Regan certainly made the figure."

"And it's evident that she used a cripple as her model. It was doubtless the vendor's child."

"Then the man who sold it must have been Pat Closky," Jean cried. "He is now taking care of Nellie Brice's baby, and though he is using an assumed name, is very likely her husband."

"And it isn't at all improbable that Pat is harboring Nina Regan!" Louise added.

Mrs. Grantland, who had been listening closely to the animated discussion, could not restrain a smile. While Jean and Louise were reasoning like a couple of veteran detectives, the older woman doubted that the puzzling bits of the mystery could be pieced together so easily.

"You must remember that Mrs. Selzer told us Nellie Brice is a widow," she said.

"Yes," Louise acknowledged. "But Nellie Brice may not have told the truth about herself. Even the matron was unaware until today that the young woman had a child."

"That's true," Mrs. Grantland admitted.

"It seems reasonable to suppose that either Nellie's surname or that of Pat Closky has been assumed," Jean said. "I believe, too, that if we were able to locate Pat, we might clear up the mystery of what happened to Nina."

"Then what would you do?" Mrs. Grantland asked, carefully steering her car to the side of the road to avoid striking a dog. "Turn her over to the authorities? Would you want her to be put into solitary confinement?"

Louise and Jean looked troubled.

"Oh, I guess it's just as well to forget all about it," Louise sighed. "It seems a pity we can't help her when she is able to make such beautiful things."

Mrs. Grantland brought the girls to Starhurst in ample time for dinner. As they entered they encountered Lettie Briggs who was loitering in the hall. Save for an enigmatic smile, she gave them no sign of recognition.

The Dana girls hurried to their rooms for hasty showers and a change of clothing. A few minutes before the dinner gong sounded Doris Harland came in to show them an afternoon newspaper.

"Here's some news you'll be interested in, Louise."

"What?"

"It's about your friend, Warden Norton."

"Friend, did you say?"

"He's in the hospital," Doris stated, "recovering from injuries he received in an automobile accident. Nothing serious, however."

"I wish," said Louise emphatically as she combed her hair, "that while he is there the doctors would give him a mental examination. I'm sure that he is unbalanced."

"I came to see you girls about another matter as well," Doris began, but the ringing of the dinner gong brought the conversation to an abrupt end. "I'll tell you about it later," she ended hastily.

As Jean and Louise filed into the dining hall with the other students, they noted that curious glances were cast in their direction. Louise even imagined that some of the girls were whispering about her and her sister. During dinner this conviction grew upon her.

"What's the matter with us, anyway?" she whispered to Jean. "Everyone acts as if we'd broken out with smallpox, or something!"

"The girls are behaving oddly. I started to talk about our trip to Pinecrest, and everyone at the table looked so extremely mysterious that I stopped."

The Dana girls were on their way to their rooms after the meal when Evelyn Starr overtook them.

"Do you know what that horrid Lettie is saying all over school?" their friend demanded.

"What?" Jean questioned.

"That you and Louise went to Pinecrest Reformatory to see a *relative*."

"So that's why the girls looked at us so curiously!" Jean cried.

"It's such an outright falsehood, too," Louise added indignantly.

"I have never before heard of such a mean trick!" Jean exclaimed, her anger increasing. "I'm going to see Lettie at once!"

Before Louise could stop her, the impulsive Jean had darted off in search of the Briggs girl. The latter was entertaining a group with her fictitious tale.

"Oh, yes, it's absolutely true," she maintained. "Jean and Louise tried to keep it a secret, but they went to Pinecrest to visit one of their near relatives. I think it was an aunt."

"Lettie Briggs! What are you saying?"

Lettie whirled about to face the furious Jean. A tell-tale flush crept over the unfriendly girl's face, for she had not expected to be caught deliberately in such a brazen falsehood.

"I heard every word you said," Jean went on, as Lettie stood by, mute. "You know very well that it isn't true. Louise and I went along with Mrs. Grantland, who is interested in social service work."

"We never did believe the story," said one of the girls.

"I only repeated what I heard," Lettie mumbled.

"You just made it up. If you don't rescind the story, I'll speak to Mrs. Crandall about it."

A look of fear flickered over Lettie's face. She could not afford to be brought before the headmistress again. She had entirely too many black marks against her record as it was.

"Oh, all right," she drawled sarcastically. "I retract everything. I'm sorry."

The apology, grudgingly given, satisfied Jean. After all, it was not in her nature to be unforgiving.

Jean's friends, however, did not feel as charitably inclined. They were incensed at the falsehood which had been circulated around the school.

"This should dispel any qualms we might have had about playing that joke on Lettie—the one we planned for her birthday," Evelyn declared. "I'm in favor of going through with it."

"So am I," Louise agreed. "We can get the ring tomorrow."

The following day the Dana girls and two of their friends made a special trip to Penfield's ten-cent store, where they purchased a ring set with the largest glass diamond they could find. After that they bought a velvet case from a well known jeweler.

"If Lettie is as little of a connoisseur of precious stones as I think she is, this should fool her," Jean chuckled.

"I can hardly wait until her birthday," Doris Harland laughed. "I guess it's fortunate that I'm going home for the week-end, for I might give away the secret."

"Lucky girl, to be spending several days at Crystal Lake again," Jean said enviously.

"Why don't you and Louise come with me?" Doris asked suddenly. "That's what I wanted to speak about last night."

During the past summer Mr. and Mrs. Harland had purchased a cottage at Crystal Lake, which was a resort not many miles distant from Penfield. For weeks Doris had been urging the Dana girls to visit there with her. Glowing accounts of the good times to be had along the waterfront had filled Louise and Jean with an overpowering desire to be her guests.

"Why not?" the younger Dana asked, turning hopefully to her sister. "I'm sure Mrs. Crandall will grant us permission."

"It would be loads of fun," Louise said enthusiastically.

"Father will come for us in the car," Doris explained. "I'll write him tonight."

The school principal readily consented to the trip when she learned that Mr. Harland would accompany the girls to Crystal Lake. Eagerly they awaited his arrival.

"Crystal Lake can't be very far from that hermitage I visited," Louise remarked in the presence of Jean and Doris.

"We pass directly through Clairtown," Jean said. She was consulting a road map, and as she did so she gave her sister an inquiring glance. "I don't suppose you'd care to go back there after your experience."

"Yes, I'd like to very much. I'm entirely over my fear of the place now. I want to return, and again thank the kind hermit who saved my life."

"We could stop on our way to Crystal Lake," Doris suggested. "Do you think you could find the place?"

"Oh, very easily," Louise returned confidently.

"Then by all means let's go there," Jean urged.

Ever since the night of Louise's disappearance she had been obsessed with a desire to see the hermitage in broad daylight. Now she was delighted that her sister was willing to return.

On Saturday morning Mr. Harland called at Starhurst for the three girls, promising Mrs. Crandall to bring them back in time for their Monday morning classes. He readily assented to their request to visit the retreat in the woods.

They drove through Clairtown, continuing along the main highway until they came to a dense thicket. Louise pointed out the curve where she thought Warden Norton's car had gone off the road. Then they proceeded to park their machine near by.

"It's only a short walk through the forest," Louise said. "The hermitage can't be very far away."

Mr. Harland and the girls set off through the dense timberland. They could find no trace of the shallow well into which Louise had fallen, nor were they able to locate any building remotely resembling the hermitage.

"Things don't look the same now as they did that night," Louise complained. "But I'm certain that this is the right place."

Mr. Harland glanced significantly at his watch. They had spent nearly half an hour in the search. He was impatient to continue on to Crystal Lake, for he had an appointment with several fishing cronies.

"Perhaps we should give it up today," he suggested.

"I suppose so," Louise agreed in disappointment. "I was so certain I could walk directly to the house."

They retraced their steps to the road, and soon found themselves speeding on to Crystal Lake.

"I still think I made no mistake about the location," Louise remarked determinedly to Jean. "Some day, when we have more time, I mean to go back and find that hermitage!"

CHAPTER X

The Carnival Man

Mr. Harland drew the car up before an attractive white cottage on the lake front. Through the magnificent willow trees Louise and Jean caught a glimpse of a lake of crystal blue water. A sailboat and a speed craft were tied up at the wharf.

"All out," the driver called cheerfully. "This is the end of the line."

Mrs. Harland had seen the automobile as it arrived, and came down the stone walk to greet the girls.

"How glad I am that you could come," she said to Jean and Louise.

"Is there anything special going on this week-end?" Doris inquired hopefully.

"No dances, I am afraid," replied her mother. "But you have arrived in time for a water carnival tomorrow. The town is having some sort of a celebration, and asked the summer cottage owners who are lingering on to help entertain visitors. Your father and I have entered a float. But thus far we haven't had time to decorate the speedboat."

"Let Jean and me help," Louise urged. "It would be fun."

"I'll turn the entire job over to you if you like," Mrs. Harland smiled. "I am very incompetent at that sort of thing myself. I have no artistic ability whatsoever."

The Dana girls were delighted to take full charge of making the float. They had both studied art at Starhurst, and enjoyed dabbling with water colors. Garbing themselves in gay smocks as became two typical young artists, they set to work with a will, permitting their love of brilliant shades to be expressed in unusual designs.

They were not satisfied with any ordinary form of decoration, so decided to dress the speedboat as a wicked monster of the sea. For three hours they were busy with crêpe paper, wire, paint and bunting. In the end they were more than pleased with the result of their handiwork.

"You certainly deserve to win after spending all that time and energy," Mrs. Harland praised. "If the entry is among the winners, you girls must take the prize."

"We did it because we enjoyed it," Louise protested. "The prize should go to you."

Doris insisted that one of the Dana girls should have the honor of piloting the craft in the parade, but they both firmly declined. The three were still debating the question when they went for a dip in the lake. The water was far too cold for comfort, and a short swim satisfied everyone. Louise and Jean preferred to stretch out on the warm sand.

The girls were abroad early the next morning, for the festival was scheduled to begin at nine. First came the speedboat races, and then the sailing events, which were indeed fascinating. As the hour drew near for the parade of floats, the crowd along the shore steadily increased. The Dana girls were glad to avoid the jam by remaining aboard the Harland entry. They cast an appraising glance over the other boats, which were lined up awaiting the signal to start down the lake.

"I think ours is the most elaborate float of all," Doris declared loyally.

"I hope it wins," Louise said, "but I'm afraid it won't. That red, white, and blue one near shore is a beauty."

Presently the signal was given for the parade to start down the lake. Doris took the wheel. As the boat passed the judges she was so nervous that her hands shook.

"It's over now," Louise said a minute later. "You'll soon know the result."

Fifteen minutes later the suspense ended with the word that the boat Doris piloted had won first prize. Mrs. Harland herself brought the good news.

"We never would have won if Louise and Jean hadn't decorated the craft," she smiled. "You must accept a portion of the prize money."

The girls demurred, but Mrs. Harland thrust a five-dollar bill into a hand of each of them.

"Of course you must take it," she laughed. "Use it in having a good time today at the carnival."

The shore near the town was lined with concessions. Barkers were calling their wares, enticing nickels and dimes from sightseekers. Doris and the Dana girls walked up and down the length of the stands trying to decide just where they should spend their money.

"I think I'll start in by buying a hamburger sandwich and one of those gigantic glasses of lemonade," Louise decided. "All that cruising on the lake gave me an appetite."

She walked slowly toward the indicated stall, assuming that Doris and Jean would follow her. When she looked around to see what had become of them, they were moving off in another direction. They wanted to see the tents of a small circus, which was one of the main attractions of the festival.

Louise ordered the sandwich, ate it leisurely, and then sauntered toward the circus grounds. A minute later she was startled to see Doris and Jean fairly running through the crowd. They were gasping for breath when they reached her.

"What's the matter?" Louise said, laughing. "Afraid of the wild animals?"

Jean brushed aside the remark. "We've just seen him, Louise!" she cried excitedly.

"Who?"

"The vendor with the statues! I'm sure he's the same man who called at the tearoom."

"What makes you think so?" Louise asked with provoking calmness.

"Because the statues look just like those we've already seen."

"Where is he now?"

"Doris and I saw him over by the lion cages. He had two figures in his hand, and I think he was trying to sell them."

"Lead me to him!" Louise commanded. "We'll not let him escape without subjecting him to the good old Dana third degree."

The girls pushed through the crowd, which had gathered near the circus tents. Presently Jean gripped her sister's hands as she caught a glimpse of the stranger.

"There he is, Louise. Do you suppose he is connected in any way with Nina Regan?"

For a full minute Louise stared at the man without saying a word. Jean grew impatient.

"Do you think we've made a mistake?"

"No, I don't. I was just a bit startled, for I'm almost certain I've seen that man before."

"Where?" Jean demanded.

"At the hermitage. I believe he is the same one who rescued me from the well."

"Then by all means let's go over and talk to him."

"All right," Louise agreed. "I'd like to question him."

The vendor was some distance from them. To reach him the girls were forced to elbow their way through the crowd which had congregated near the entrance to the circus tent.

"Now, if he doesn't get away before we reach him—" Louise began, but the words froze upon her lips.

There was a sudden commotion from within the tent. A woman screamed. Like a great wave the crowd surged back from the entrance.

"Run for your lives!" went up the cry. "A tiger is loose!"

CHAPTER XI

A Daring Act

THE tiger, a vicious looking beast which had escaped from its cage within the circus tent, dashed directly into the milling crowd. Women screamed and fled in terror. Children were trampled upon as they sought to escape.

Louise and Jean saw to their dismay that the beast was heading straight for the vendor of statues.

"Look out! Look out!" Louise screamed.

The peddler was well aware of his danger, but stood his ground unflinchingly. As the tiger poised ready to spring, the man raised one of his statues and hurled it at the beast. The vendor's aim was not good and missed the animal by inches.

Jean, however, was standing directly in the path of the flying missile. She attempted to duck, but was too late. The statue struck her a glancing blow on the head. She staggered back and fell to the ground.

"Jean! Jean!" Louise cried frantically, trying to reach her sister and protect her from being trampled on by the crowd.

Fortunately the girl had not been seriously injured by the blow. It had merely stunned her momentarily, causing her to lose her balance.

A real danger confronted her now. The tiger's attention had been diverted from the vendor, who had fled in terror as soon as he had thrown the statue. The animal saw the girl lying on the ground and leaped toward her.

Women fainted. Everybody expected to see Jean torn to pieces by the enraged beast. Louise made a desperate effort to get between her sister and the tiger, but the crowd held her back.

It was all over in an instant. Jean saw the animal rushing down upon her. She hurled at it the only thing she had in her hand—a box of chocolates purchased a few minutes before.

Her aim was true. The carton struck the tiger squarely in the jaws. Pieces of candy spilled over the ground.

The attacker hesitated, sniffed, and then began to lick one of the chocolates. This gave Jean the opportunity she needed to scramble to her feet.

By this time, several circus employees had arrived upon the scene with pistols and ropes. While the beast stood licking the chocolates, the attendants were able to lasso it with ropes and drop a cage down over it.

"Jean! You might have been killed!" Louise gasped. Of the two girls she was the more nervous. "Oh, your forehead is bleeding!"

"It's only a tiny scratch and doesn't hurt," Jean maintained. "The statue struck me, I guess."

"It was brave of you to throw the box of chocolates the way you did," Doris Harland praised. "I was so stunned I couldn't even move!"

"It was lucky for me that the tiger had an appetite for sweets," Jean laughed shakily. "Otherwise, I might be making a nice meal for him now."

"Don't joke about it," Louise pleaded. "You had such a narrow escape from death, Jean."

"I know I did," her sister acknowledged soberly.

The crowd surged about the girls admiringly. Jean grew embarrassed at the attention of curious onlookers. Her clothes were dirty and torn.

"Let's get away from here," she said in an undertone.

"You must go back to the cottage and have that scratch treated," Louise told her sternly.

A policeman made an aisle through the onlookers. In their haste to get away, the Danas did not notice that Doris was not with them.

"What became of her?" Louise asked in surprise, looking back. "She was with us a minute ago."

"She probably was caught in the crowd. Let's go on. Doris will know where we are."

Mrs. Harland was not at the cottage when they got there, but the girls found everything they needed in the medicine cabinet. Jean's forehead was neatly bandaged by the time Doris arrived.

"What delayed you?" Louise questioned. "We lost you somewhere in the crowd."

For answer Doris triumphantly held up two statues. The Danas uttered a shriek of delight.

"How did you get them?" Jean demanded.

"The vendor left them when he fled. I tried to get the one he hurled at the tiger, but I'm afraid it was smashed."

"I think you're right about that," Jean agreed, ruefully feeling her forehead.

"I was so eager to get Sis away that I never once remembered the figures," Louise said eagerly. "It was lucky you thought of them, Doris."

The girl flushed at the praise. It had always been her ambition to assist the Dana girls in solving a mystery.

"Let me look at the sculpturing," Jean requested.

Doris willingly handed the figures to her. One of the statues was that of a child's head, the other that of a hooded monk.

"They do look like Nina Regan's work," Jean declared.

She turned them over, and there, initialed in the base of each, were the letters "N. R."

"Oh, I wish we could have questioned that vendor!" Louise exclaimed. "He might have been able to explain a great many things which have baffled us in this case."

"I looked for him in the crowd after the tiger was captured," Doris said, "but he wasn't there. I waited a few minutes for him to return for his statues. Then I decided to bring them along with me."

"If you hadn't done so, some other person would have walked off with them," Louise said. "We may be able to find him, and return his property."

Jean insisted that she felt strong enough to begin the search immediately. As soon as she had donned fresh clothing, the girls walked back to the circus grounds in search of the vendor, but he was nowhere to be seen. They inquired for him at several stands along the waterfront without success. The man had disappeared.

"It's of no use," Jean sighed in disappointment as they returned late in the afternoon to the cottage. "That old tiger ruined everything!"

"Well, at least Doris has two fine statues," Louise remarked cheerfully.

"I want you girls to take them," she said quickly. "I don't care about them."

"But they are very fine pieces," Jean protested. "You rescued them, Doris, and you should be the one to keep them."

"I have never cared much for bric-a-brac. Besides, these works might be of some use to you and Louise. You'll do me a favor by accepting them."

In the end Louise and Jean agreed to Doris's wishes in the matter. The little statuettes would serve as a memento of their week-end visit at Crystal Lake.

During the remainder of their stay the Dana girls tried in every way possible to locate the missing vendor. When all attempts had failed, they agreed that he must have left town. All too soon it came time for the girls to return to Starhurst. Reluctantly they packed their bags.

"I'm not going to risk breaking our valuables," Louise said. "I'll wrap each of them by itself."

She found some tissue paper, and after carefully covering both pieces, brought them downstairs and placed them on the back porch, where their traveling bags were.

"Just leave everything here, and Father will put the luggage in the car when he brings it over from the garage," Doris directed.

The Dana girls went back into the cottage to say good-bye to Mrs. Harland, and to thank her for their enjoyable week-end visit. Fifteen minutes later they heard the automobile at the door, and went outside to see if Mr. Harland was ready to leave.

"Why, whatever became of our statues?" Jean inquired in surprise as she stepped onto the rear porch. "We left them here beside the bags, didn't we, Louise?"

"Yes, I put them there myself."

Louise stared in blank astonishment. Although the luggage was still standing there, the two figures were gone!

CHAPTER XII

THE FAKE DIAMOND

"THE statues must be here somewhere," Doris insisted when the Dana girls told her of their loss. "Father may have put them in the car."

She went to inquire, but Mr. Harland declared that he had taken nothing from the porch.

"Then the figures *were* stolen," Jean wailed. "Oh, dear, if that isn't the worst luck ever!"

"I cannot imagine who could have taken them," Doris said in perplexity.

They saw no one walking away from the grounds, nor was there a single clue as to the identity of the thief. It was the first time anything had been stolen from the Harlands while at Crystal Lake. They were so distressed over the loss that the Dana girls forced themselves to make light of it.

"After all, the statues really didn't belong to us," Louise said, as she bade her hostess good-bye. "Please don't give the matter another thought, Mrs. Harland."

The luggage was placed in the car, and a

few minutes later the girls were speeding back to their school. Louise and Jean had been hoping that on the return trip they might stop near Clairtown to search once more for the hermitage. However, they had left Crystal Lake later than they had intended, and dared not delay long on the road if they hoped to arrive at Starhurst for early morning classes. Nevertheless, at Louise's suggestion Mr. Harland pulled up at a filling station to inquire of the attendant if he knew of such a place located in the vicinity.

"Never heard of one," the man responded. "I've lived around here for ten years, too."

It seemed useless to search further after that, but Louise still clung to the belief that the hermitage was hidden deep in the woods.

"Some day, when I have plenty of time, I'm coming back here and find it," she whispered to Jean. "And I intend to learn its secret, too!"

The girls arrived at Starhurst in ample time for their classes. Despite the fact that they had been away over the week-end, they had prepared their lessons, and did not fall down in their recitations. Lettie, on the other hand, stumbled through the passage of French which she was translating, and was severely reprimanded before the entire class.

"I suppose you were thinking about that big diamond ring your parents are going to give you for your birthday," one of the students jibed after the session was over. "Are you really to get such a large jewel?"

"I certainly am," the girl returned haughtily. "It will be the nicest ring that money can buy, too."

Lettie's parents were rich, but no one had ever determined the exact extent of their wealth. She herself maintained that her father had made more than ten million dollars in oil. However, her stories were always questioned by her hearers, and this amount was minimized considerably by the students.

Unaware that the Dana girls and their friends were planning a joke at her expense, Lettie played directly into their hands by talking almost constantly of the fine birthday present she was to receive. Furthermore, she did not suspect that anything was brewing when a small package was delivered to her door on the eve of her birthday.

"It's my ring!" she exclaimed to Ina Mason.

Without even glancing at the writing on the outside, Lettie tore off the paper and opened the velvet case. She was decidedly impressed with the size of the diamond. It was the largest stone of its kind she had ever seen.

"Won't the Dana girls be green-eyed with jealousy when they see this!" she cried. "Isn't it beautiful?"

"Gorgeous," Ina agreed. She added dubiously, "It doesn't seem to sparkle as much as some diamonds I've seen, though."

"That's because of the poor light," Lettie said sharply. She turned on extra illumination. "Now, you see!" she exclaimed.

"Of course," her toady agreed meekly. She knew better than to argue with Lettie.

"I'm going to show it to the girls, Ina. It will be fun to watch their eyes get as big as saucers."

Lettie was pleased to find the Danas and a number of their friends lingering in the lower hall.

"Well, how do you like my birthday present?" she asked proudly, waving her hand about for them to see. "Isn't the diamond as big as I said it would be?"

"Oh, much larger," Jean returned soberly as she bent over to inspect it. "But Lettie, you don't mean to tell us this is your birthday ring?"

"Certainly it is."

"I thought you said your father was sending you a diamond," Louise said innocently.

"What do you think this is? A ruby?"

"It looks to me as if it might be glass."

"Glass!" Lettie fairly screamed the word. "You dare to say my father would send me a glass ring?"

"It doesn't sparkle," Evelyn Starr pointed out, trying to keep from laughing.

"I don't believe the band is gold," Jean interposed. "See? It rubs off green, and real gold won't do that."

Lettie snatched her hand away angrily. "Oh, you make me tired!" she muttered. "I won't believe this ring isn't genuine, though you'd like me to. I'll write my father and prove it!"

Her confidence was greatly shaken, but she was too proud to show it. Everywhere she flaunted the diamond.

The morning mail brought Lettie a small insured package from her parents. By prearrangement, the Dana girls and their friends were at hand when it arrived. Lettie's face flushed a deep scarlet on seeing it. For the first time she suspected a hoax.

"Why don't you open your present?" Doris Harland urged mischievously. "It looks as if it might contain another diamond ring."

Lettie would have preferred to refuse; yet, when the other students joined Doris in urging her to show them its contents, she could not escape. Reluctantly she removed the wrappings to disclose the jewel her parents had sent her.

It was a tiny diamond, no larger than the one in Doris Harland's wrist watch. A ripple of amusement swept over the group of girls.

"I guess the Danas were right," Evelyn chuckled. "The other ring was a fake. You didn't buy it yourself to impress us, did you, Lettie?"

"No, I didn't!"

The Briggs girl glared angrily at Jean and Louise. Although she could not prove it, she suspected that they were responsible for her extreme embarrassment. Jerking the cheap jewelry from her finger, she flung it across the hall. Then she ran to her room and locked the door.

The Danas decided that the joke had been carried far enough, so passed along the word that Lettie was not to be reminded of the incident again. Nevertheless, for weeks to come diamonds were a sensitive topic of conversation to the girl. It was days before she would even wear the gift of her parents.

The mail which resulted in Lettie's chagrin brought an interesting letter addressed to Louise. She and Jean decided to open it in their rooms.

"I have no idea whom it's from," Louise admitted, as she scanned the unfamiliar writing on the envelope.

"Then hurry up and find out before I die of curiosity," Jean urged.

As Louise slit the envelope, a sheet of paper fluttered to the floor. It had been torn from a tablet, and the brief message on it had been written with a pencil.

"Dear Miss Dana," the note said. "I took my statues from the back porch because I saw them there. I knew that you and your sister did not intend to steal them."

The note was signed "Street Vendor."

"Why, what a strange note," Jean exclaimed. "Why didn't the man use his real name?"

"And how did he learn mine?"

"He may have inquired at Crystal Lake."

"Only the Harlands know us there, Jean. I think it's significant that he addressed the letter to me instead of to you. I am beginning to suspect this street vendor is the same man who helped me out of the well."

"Perhaps," Jean agreed doubtfully. "Anyway, I'm glad the statues are in the hands of their rightful owner."

With their minds distracted by the mystery which surrounded Nina Regan and the strange hermit, it was surprising that the Dana girls did any studying at all. Louise became almost obsessed with the idea of returning to the hermitage.

Days passed before she had an opportunity to look for the place again. It came when Professor Crandall mentioned casually to a group of students one day that he was delivering a lecture on Greek Mythology before a number of educators who were to hold a conference the following week at Clairtown. Louise nudged her sister, and said in most flattering tones:

"Jean and I should like very much to hear your talk, Professor Crandall. Your subject is closely related to a term paper I am preparing."

"Would you really care to go?" the man beamed. "Perhaps it can be arranged. I'll speak to my wife about it."

When Mr. Crandall had moved on to the office, Jean said to her sister, "Do you think I want to sit through a tedious lecture on Greek mythology?"

"Why not?" Louise laughed. "It will give us a chance to look for the hermitage."

"I suppose we'll have to hunt for it around the lecture hall!"

"We'll find some way of doing it, Jean. Leave everything to me."

The girls were highly pleased when Professor Crandall met them after English class the following day, and told them he had arranged for them to accompany him to Clairtown. They thanked him demurely, and were discreet enough to keep their plans strictly to themselves.

On the way to the conference, Louise tried

to figure out the best way of broaching to Professor Crandall her desire to search for the hermitage. Finally she decided that it would be best to tell him the truth about the matter.

"Well, well," the old gentleman said, a twinkle in his eyes, "so my lecture wasn't the real attraction of the trip? I must confess I suspected that from the first."

Jean and Louise had the grace to look serious.

"I'm sure we'll enjoy and profit from your talk," Jean commented politely.

"Girls are all alike," the professor sighed. "Expose them to the benefits of education, and they do not appreciate their opportunities. Now, when I was a boy——"

He launched into a lengthy account of his struggle to acquire an education. When he had finished, he said kindly:

"Never mind, you shall visit your hermitage. During the social hour which follows my address, you may take the car and run away by yourselves."

"Oh, thank you, Mr. Crandall," Jean said, smiling.

"Mind, not a word of this to Mrs. Crandall," the professor warned. "She may think I have given you too much liberty."

"We'll be very discreet," Louise promised.

At the auditorium where the lecture was to

be given, the Dana girls found seats far back. The audience was slow in gathering, so that the meeting started late. Finally Professor Crandall was introduced. Always inclined to be prolix, he threatened to consume the entire afternoon. At last, however, the lecture came to an end amid loud applause.

So many persons gathered about the speaker that the Dana girls could not get near him for several minutes. Then he smiled as he caught sight of them.

"Here are the car keys, Louise," he said, taking them from his pocket. "Be sure to drive carefully, and try to be back here in an hour."

The girls fairly flew to the parking lot.

"We'll have to step on it if we hope to make it," Jean said. "Better let me drive."

"All right, I can watch the road for landmarks."

They drove out of Clairtown, and at Louise's suggestion selected a side road they had not been over before. It, too, wound through the forest.

"Somehow, this part looks more familiar," Louise commented. "I believe Warden Norton must have taken me along this route. I remember that the road was rough."

They had traveled but a short distance, when Louise told her sister to stop the car.

"Let's park here and hike through the woods. I believe this is the place."

Jean drove to the side of the road, and the two girls abandoned the car, making their way carefully through the dense timber.

"Yes, this is right!" Louise cried a minute later. "We're coming to the well."

As they did so, they paused to look down into it, then hurried on.

"We can't be very far from the hermitage now," the older girl said hopefully.

Presently they came to a trail which they decided to follow. To their delight, it led them directly to the lonely cabin. They were but a hundred yards away from it, when Jean suddenly halted, holding up her hand for silence.

Both girls paused, listening. They could hear footsteps. Someone was following them down the trail!

The two sisters stepped hastily into the bushes, and waited as a man came into view. He was the street vendor! Without seeing them, he walked directly past the girls and entered the little house.

"There, didn't I tell you!" Louise exclaimed triumphantly. "I knew he was the hermit!"

"You seem to be right. That makes the case more baffling than ever."

While the girls were debating as to their next move, the door of the hermitage opened.

The man came out, tenderly holding a crippled child in his arms.

Louise and Jean watched, breathless, as the vendor placed a blanket and some pillows on the ground, and gently placed the child on the improvised bed.

"The sunshine will do you good," they heard him murmur. "It will make those poor twisted bones grow strong and straight."

Tears brimmed in Jean's eyes. She could hardly bear to look at the pathetic little form.

"Shall we go over and talk to him?" Louise asked softly.

Jean nodded, but before the Danas could leave their hiding-place, they were startled at hearing a crackling noise in the underbrush.

"Someone else is coming," Jean whispered.

They drew back into their retreat. A minute later Ex-Warden Norton appeared. He paused not more than ten feet from the place where the girls were hiding.

They saw him bend down and pick up a club from the ground. Then, with a wild look in his eyes, he stole down the trail toward the hermitage!

CHAPTER XIII

A New Discovery

From their lookout among the bushes, Jean and Louise saw the ex-warden confront the vendor.

"Where have you hidden Nina Regan?" he fairly shouted, brandishing the club menacingly.

Taken completely by surprise, the old man sprang to his feet, an expression of fear flashing over his face. When he replied, his voice was so low that the girls could not hear what he said. But the warden's growing anger was unmistakable.

"You can't fool me, Pat Closky," he cried furiously. "I'd know you in any disguise. That crippled child is Nellie Brice's, too."

Louise gripped Jean's hand tightly. The revelation was a thrilling one, and confirmed their own deductions. They waited with bated breaths.

"Where is Nina Regan?" the warden repeated, raising his club over the vendor's head. "Tell me, or I'll——"

"I've already said that I can't tell you," the

111

old man answered in distress. "Put down that stick and leave me in peace."

"I'll leave you with a cracked skull," Norton muttered. "Come on, out with it. Where have you hidden the girl?"

"Search the cottage if you like, but you won't find her here!"

The offensive man decided to accept the challenge. Club in hand, he cautiously entered the weird abode. No sooner had he vanished inside than the vendor quietly slipped into the hermitage after him.

"Our friend, the warden, has walked into a trap," Louise commented wisely.

"It looks that way," Jean said.

They were correct. A little later the noise of shouting and pounding came from within the building. Apparently Norton was attempting to break down a door.

"He has been locked in," Jean chuckled. "It serves him right, too." The vendor emerged into the clearing a moment later, smiling to himself. Disregarding the commotion within the hermitage, he went over to the child who had begun to whimper with fear.

Gently he massaged the infant's wasted limbs, smiling all the while. The shouts from within the cabin grew louder, but he paid no attention to them.

"What shall we do now?" Jean asked in

perplexity. "If we go over and speak to the man, he'll know that we've seen everything."

"We might wait a few minutes and find out what happens."

Jean glanced at her wrist watch.

"We can't do that, either. We've been away from Clairtown almost an hour already."

"I can hardly believe it!"

"Yes. If we intend to keep our promise to Professor Crandall, we'll have to start back at once."

"Oh, dear, just when things are growing so exciting!"

"At least, we've made several valuable discoveries, Louise."

"Yes, and when we tell Professor Crandall what we have seen he may agree to return here with us." Louise cast an anxious glance toward the hermitage. "I don't like to leave now. If that man Norton should get out of the locked room, there's no telling what he may do," she said in a worried voice.

"I think the best thing for us to do is to go for help."

The girls were separated from the main trail by a tiny clearing. In order to reach the protection of the woods, they would have to cross this piece of ground.

"How can we get away without Mr. Closky seeing us?" Jean questioned. "If we move out of these bushes we'll be directly in his line of vision.''

The Dana girls feared that they were in a trap of their own making. However, as the pounding from within the cabin increased in violence, Closky arose. Leaving the crippled child lying upon the lawn, he again entered the house.

''Now is our chance,'' Louise whispered.

The instant the door of the hermitage closed behind the vendor, the girls slipped into the forest and ran as fast as they could over to the parked automobile.

''Full speed ahead!'' Jean commanded crisply, as her sister took the wheel.

Ten minutes of fast driving brought them into Clairtown, where Professor Crandall was waiting on the steps of the auditorium building. He had been pacing nervously back and forth.

''You're three minutes late,'' he announced. ''I had begun to fear something had gone wrong.''

Tensely Louise and Jean told him what they had witnessed at the hermitage. When they had finished, they pleaded with their escort to return with them. To their astonishment he seemed unwilling to do so.

''It would be far better to call in the authorities,'' he maintained.

"Oh, you don't understand, Professor Crandall," Louise cried anxiously. "We can't do that. If the police question Pat Closky they'll be almost certain to get some trace of Nina Regan."

"Isn't she a fugitive from justice?" the professor asked stiffly. "If my memory serves me correctly, her crime was a serious one, too."

Louise and Jean almost gasped. At times Professor Crandall could be provokingly deliberate. In detail they repeated to him everything connected with the Regan case.

"Nina's guilt was never proven," Jean ended. "She was convicted purely on circumstantial evidence."

"Please come back with us, Professor Crandall," Louise pleaded. "If not for Nina Regan's sake, then for the sake of that poor crippled child."

"Very well," he finally consented, "but I must say it is decidedly contrary to my better judgment."

He insisted upon driving the car himself, going along at such a moderate pace that Jean and Louise had difficulty in concealing their impatience. Moments were so precious! Almost anything could happen to Pat Closky during their absence.

The professor parked his automobile in the identical spot where Louise and Jean had halted a short time before. Scarcely had the motor been switched off, than they heard someone come crashing through the underbrush.

"Wait!" Louise cautioned, as Professor Crandall started to get out of the car.

The next instant Ex-Warden Norton came into view, running as fast as he could.

"Why, he has escaped!" Jean exclaimed.

"I wonder if Closky let him go, or if he broke away himself," Louise added anxiously.

Without even glancing in the direction of the parked automobile, Norton darted down the road.

"We must hurry over to the hermitage," Louise declared, springing from the car. "In making his escape, that man may have harmed Pat Closky and the child! I'm sure he is crazy!"

Professor Crandall shuddered, for above everything else he abhorred violence.

"Would you care to stay here on guard," Jean suggested quickly, "while Louise and I go on alone? Warden Norton might decide to return."

The professor looked relieved.

"That is a sensible plan, I believe," he agreed. "If I see the man again I'll detain him."

Hand in hand Louise and Jean vanished into the woods.

CHAPTER XIV

THE MASQUERADER

"PROFESSOR Crandall can be more useful back there than at the hermitage," Louise said, as she and her sister darted through the forest.

They came to the clearing, and halted. The door of the hermitage was open, but neither the vendor nor the child was in sight.

"They must be indoors," Louise declared. "You wait here, Jean, while I find out."

"But I want to go, too."

"Pat Closky already knows me, Jean. If both of us pounce down upon him at the same time he may become suspicious."

"Yes, that's true. But what excuse will you offer for coming here?"

Louise paused an instant. "I'll pretend I want to buy those statues we saw at the festival, and which he took from us."

"All right, but at the first opportunity call for me to come, too."

Louise slipped from behind the trees, and walked rapidly toward the hermitage. She decided to enter by the cliff side, so was forced to circle the building.

A child's cry drew her attention toward a high, rocky ledge adjacent to the cabin. Louise's heart missed a beat! Left alone only a few minutes, the crippled child had crept on his hands and knees to the very edge of the precipice! Unaware of his danger, the youngster now stretched out its fist to pluck a wild flower which grew just over the edge.

For an instant Louise was too terrified to move. Then she sprang forward to save the babe. As she did so, Pat Closky came to the door of the hermitage. His face blanched as he beheld the scene.

Louise snatched up the child and carried it to safety. At the same time the vendor ran over and relieved the girl of her burden.

"Oh, thank you, thank you," he murmured brokenly. "I could never have forgiven myself if anything had happened to the baby."

Louise decided that this was a strategic moment in which to introduce herself, since the rescue of the child had placed her in a most favorable light.

"I am Louise Dana," she explained. "You doubtless recall that I stayed over night here at your home not long ago."

"Yes," said the vendor noncommittally.

"My sister and I are very much interested in the statues which you sell. We thought you might be induced to part with one of them."

The old man remained silent, and Louise continued:

"My sister is waiting. I'll call her." She signaled toward the trees.

Jean, who had been eagerly watching, instantly emerged. As Louise introduced her to the vendor, she stared at him in surprise.

"Why, you bear a marked resemblance to my sister!" she exclaimed.

The comment was as embarrassing to Louise as it was to Pat Closky, yet it was true. There was a decided similarity in their features. Despite the vendor's clothing and bushy, gray hair, he had a young face and certain feminine characteristics. He fondled the child as a woman would, and his voice was high-pitched.

"You are Nina Regan in disguise!" Jean suddenly cried out, before Louise could speak.

"Nina Regan! You accuse me of being a woman!" The vendor laughed shakily.

"You have the hands of a woman!" Louise exclaimed. "And your voice! You may as well admit your identity."

The man suddenly burst into tears.

"Yes, I am Nina Regan," the masquerader sobbed. "Until you came today no one has suspected the truth. I've been very happy here in this hermitage."

"How long have you been living at this place?" Louise inquired kindly.

"Ever since I escaped from Pinecrest Reformatory. Now that my secret is known, I fear I shall have to go back to that life of torment! And yet I am innocent!"

Jean and Louise eyed each other uneasily. The situation was not to their liking. Obviously, as good citizens it would be their duty to turn Nina Regan over to the authorities; yet they had no desire to do so.

"I've never committed a crime in my life," Nina continued, weeping. "I always liked Mrs. Keating, who was my employer, and I wouldn't have harmed her for the world."

"Was there no way whereby you could prove your innocence?" Jean asked.

"I had no money with which to engage lawyers. Even so, I think the case might have been dropped had it not been for a distant relative of Mrs. Keating, who pressed the charges against me," Nina Regan explained.

"Without regard for the evidence, I suppose," Louise commented.

"Yes. And the authorities didn't help to keep me from a conviction. After that it was my cruel misfortune to be sentenced to Pinecrest Reformatory. Warden Norton hated me from the first, and never once gave me a chance. He resented my friendship with Nellie Brice."

"Isn't this Nellie's child?" Jean inquired.

"Yes. When we were at Pinecrest together

I promised her that I would care for the little
girl until she should be free. I've done the
best I possibly could. I've fashioned and sold
statues to keep us in food. Recently I managed to scrape together enough money to pay
for special medical treatment for the child. I
had hoped—but what's the use?"

"Please go on," Louise urged very gently.
"We're really interested."

Nina Regan studied their faces intently, almost hopefully.

"You didn't come here with Warden Norton,
did you?" she demanded.

"Absolutely not," Louise replied. "We have
no more liking for that man than you have."

"You weren't sent to question me, then?"

"No, we came of our own accord," Jean assured her. "Louise wanted to thank you for
saving her life when she fell into the well. And
we were both interested in your beautiful
statues."

A fleeting smile lighted up the sculptress's
face. "I love my art," she said. Her eyes
roved over the limestone cliffs. "Material to
work with is always available, and this peace-
ful hermitage is an ideal place in which to
model."

"You are a genius!" Jean burst out, unable
to control her admiration.

Nina Regan smiled sadly. "I shouldn't call

myself that. In the field of art I am not even recognized.''

''But you will be some day,'' Louise stoutly maintained.

Nina shook her head. ''You forget that my name can never be known to the world. I am a fugitive from justice, with no opportunity to prove my innocence.''

As Louise and Jean remained silent, she went on with a swift change of mood.

''Well, it's over now—I have had a few months of freedom, and now I shall have to go back. You may as well call the authorities, and get everything settled.''

Tears began to well up into Nina's eyes. Louise and Jean exchanged baffled glances, not knowing just what to do. While it was true that the woman was wanted by the authorities, the girls could not believe her guilty; nor did they relish assuming the responsibility of deciding what course to pursue.

The Danas drew apart, and whispered together for a time. Then they returned to Nina. ''Stay here,'' they said kindly. ''We really want to help you, and think we can figure out a way to do it.''

''I'll wait,'' the young woman promised.

Louise and Jean hurriedly set off to consult Professor Crandall, and try to gain his approval of a daring plan which they hoped to put into effect.

CHAPTER XV

SERIOUS TROUBLE

LOUISE and Jean found Professor Crandall seated in the parked automobile where they had left him. He had grown alarmed over their continued absence, and was relieved when he saw them again.

Louise lost no time in telling him of the important discovery which she and her sister had made at the hermitage. As the story progressed, the professor's face was indeed a study.

"Just exactly what is this plan of yours?" he frowned. "Repeat it, please."

"We want to conceal Nina Regan and the child for a few days," Jean explained.

"It doesn't seem right to turn the young woman over to the authorities," Louise added.

"But my dear girls, you are plotting to thwart justice!"

"On the contrary, we hope to see a grave wrong righted," Jean affirmed. "If you would only speak to Nina Regan, I'm sure you would agree with us that she is innocent."

"But even if I should sanction this wild

123

scheme, in the end what good would result? You can't hide Nina Regan indefinitely.''

''We don't intend to do that, Professor Crandall,'' Louise said. ''We only hope to keep her under cover until she has had time in which to prove her innocence.''

''If she has been safe at the hermitage all these months, why not permit her to remain there?''

''Because Ex-Warden Norton saw her this afternoon,'' Jean explained patiently. ''While he doesn't know that Nina Regan and Pat Closky are one and the same person, he does realize that there is a close connection between them. Nina won't dare to stay there any longer, for there may be another investigation.''

''I see. While I agree with you that your purpose is a very noble one, I feel that it would. be unwise to permit you to go through with the plan.''

Jean cast her sister a despairing glance. Professor Crandall was so hopelessly cautious! He would never give his consent! Louise was equally discouraged over the man's attitude, but she was not ready to give up trying to persuade him.

''I wish you would talk to Miss Regan, Professor Crandall,'' she suggested.

''I do not doubt but that her case would move me to sympathy. That, however, is not the point. From what you have told me it appears this young woman has not had a fair trial.''

''Then why can't we help her to get one?'' Jean demanded.

''You haven't stopped to think of your own side of the matter,'' the professor cautioned. ''If the authorities should learn that you secreted this woman, you both might be prosecuted.''

Jean and Louise had failed to consider this angle, but they were not discouraged by it.

''We're willing to take the risk,'' the latter announced. ''Oh please, Professor Crandall, won't you at least talk to Nina?''

The gentleman nodded. It was difficult for him to deny the request when the Dana girls made it appear such a reasonable one. Yet he gave them his promise with reservations.

''I'll see the young woman, but mind, I haven't agreed to this wild scheme of yours. What will Mrs. Crandall say when she hears of it?''

''She will think you did the right thing, I'm sure,'' Jean said.

''Perhaps she would at that. Well, shall we have a talk with this young person?''

Jean and Louise led the way through the forest. They were light-hearted, for they believed that the kindly Mr. Crandall would come to their way of figuring when he had met Nina and talked to her.

Their discussion with the professor had consumed more time than either of the girls realized. Nearly half an hour had elapsed since they had left the hermitage.

"I hope Nina hasn't grown tired of waiting," Louise whispered to her sister. "We could have come directly back if Mr. Crandall hadn't been so cautious."

As they drew near the hermitage, the girls saw that the grounds were deserted. Thinking that Nina Regan had taken the child inside, they went to the door and knocked.

There was no response.

"That's strange," Jean remarked. "Nina promised she would wait for us."

"She may not have heard what we said."

Louise rapped again. Professor Crandall banged his fist upon the door, but no one came to open it.

Louise turned the knob, but the door was locked. However, when the professor pushed his entire weight against it, the feeble latch gave way. Then all three went in.

"I am afraid the young lady has flown," the girls' escort remarked, looking about the room.

Everywhere there was evidence of flight. Papers were scattered over the floor; garments

had been removed from hooks. Nina and the
child were gone.

Disconsolate, Jean and Louise tramped
through the hermitage. They were bitterly
disappointed in the sculptress, for they had
trusted her to keep her promise.

"I guess Professor Crandall was right after
all," Louise admitted ruefully. "We were acting hastily in deciding to help Nina before we
knew very much about her."

"By running away, she has shown that she
isn't as trustworthy as we thought," Jean acknowledged.

The hermitage consisted of three rooms. The
main chamber was the one in which Louise had
slept the night of her first visit. The empty
one adjoining it still contained the cradle where
the crippled child had lain, while the room beyond had apparently served as Nina Regan's
studio.

"I begin to understand now why I thought
the place was haunted," Louise said, pointing
to several of the sculptress's tools which had
been left behind.

"What do you mean?"

"Those tapping noises must have come from
this room. Nina was working on her statues."

"But I thought you said you saw ghostlike
forms through the trees, too."

"I must have imagined that part of it."

Jean had been peering out of the workroom window. "No, you didn't," she cried. "Tell me what you see."

"Figures carved on the rocks!" Louise exclaimed, laughing. "Well, that was a good joke on me."

"I don't wonder you were frightened almost to death, Louise. I'd have jumped a mile myself if I had seen those figures at night."

"It was foolish of me to run off, Jean. I shouldn't have done it, only my nerves were already shattered by the experiences I'd had before I reached tne hermitage."

"You must have had remarkable self-control to remain here until morning," Jean praised. "I doubt that I could have done it."

Although Nina Regan had left many of her half-finished statues behind her, she had taken with her all her clothing and that of the child. Sighting the abandoned disguise lying upon the floor, Louise picked it up, and after an instant's hesitation burned it in the fireplace.

"It's just as well that no evidence be left here," she remarked to Jean.

While the two girls stood quietly watching the flames consume the garments, Professor Crandall came in from the adjoining room to learn what was detaining them. He was eager to start for Penfield, as it was getting late.

"My wife will be greatly upset over our delay. We have wasted too much time as it is.''

"We may as well go," Louise admitted. "I'm sorry we caused you so much inconvenience, Professor Crandall.''

"Don't feel bad about it. When you are as old as I am, Louise, you will not readily place so much faith in human nature.''

The three returned to the main room. As they moved toward the door they were startled by hearing people talking in the clearing.

"Right this way, men!" bellowed a familiar voice. "Closky is probably hiding inside. Surround the place!''

Jean rushed to the window and peered cautiously out.

"It's Warden Norton," she warned in a whisper. "What shall we do?''

"You have no need to fear him while I am along," Professor Crandall assured the girls.

"I'm afraid you don't know what sort of man he is," Louise told him nervously. "Sometimes I think he isn't in his right mind.''

Jean quickly latched the door and placed a chair up against it.

"Come, come," said their escort impatiently, "there's no need for your taking such precautions. We'll go out and talk to Warden Norton.''

A loud knock sounded upon the door. "Open up!'' came the command.

"Who is it?" Professor Crandall called out.

Warden Norton's men answered the question by smashing in the door. Before the Starhurst teacher could recover from his astonishment, a burly fellow weighing at least two hundred pounds sprang upon him.

Infuriated at such treatment, Professor Crandall resisted his attacker. The two men clinched and fell to the floor, rolling over and over in their struggle.

"Oh, punch him, Mr. Crandall!" Jean shrieked excitedly, forgetting for the moment that the professor disapproved of vigorous language for young ladies.

Louise glanced quickly about the room for a weapon. As she did so, her eyes rested upon one of Nina's statues. She reached for it, but two men who had entered the hermitage with Warden Norton caught her by the arms.

"Run for help, Jean!" Louise cried.

Then she saw that her sister had also been overpowered. They were all prisoners of Warden Norton!

CHAPTER XVI

The Landslide

"What do you mean by this outrage?" gasped Professor Crandall, as he struggled to regain his feet. "Let me explain."

"You'll explain everything at headquarters," muttered the burly man who had attacked him and was now taking a pair of handcuffs from his pocket.

At sight of the fetters, the scholarly professor turned pale. With a supreme effort he threw off his assailant. The officer was on him again in an instant, for Mr. Crandall was no match for the big fellow, either in strength or skill. He was forced back against the wall, and his arm was cruelly wrenched.

"Warden Norton!" Louise cried, as that man suddenly appeared in the doorway. "Make them stop! It is all a terrible mistake!"

As the man noticed the professor and the girls, his face blanched. He realized only too well that the unprovoked attack upon this fine looking stranger and the Danas would result in serious trouble for him. He had expected to find only Nina Regan and her protectors inside the hermitage.

"I've bungled things again," was the unpleasant thought which flashed through his mind. "If this story ever gets out, I'll be ruined."

A strange, sick feeling came over him, and he staggered blindly toward a couch.

"Mr. Norton, call off your men!" Jean screamed. "Can't you see they're killing Professor Crandall?"

The warden moistened his lips. He tried to speak, but could not. A mist came over his eyes. Then he fell to the floor in a faint.

The attackers abandoned the fight for the moment. Leaving the battered professor lying limp in a corner, they hurried over to aid their leader. Jean succeeded in freeing herself from the grasp of the officer who was holding her, and ran to help Mr. Crandall.

"I'm all right," the scholarly man muttered thickly. "Get away from here if you can. Don't bother about me."

Escape was out of the question, for one of the policemen stood guard at the door of the cabin. All were working over the unconscious ex-warden save the officer who was holding Louise.

Presently Norton began to revive. To the dismay of the Dana girls he seemed to have no recollection whatsoever of what had just taken place. No sign of recognition flashed over his face as he turned his gaze toward them.

"Nina Regan," he muttered incoherently, closing his eyes, "I'll get you this time. I know you're here."

"Nina Regan is *not* here," Louise tried to explain to the officers. "She——"

The policeman would not listen to her. It was obvious that he and the other officers believed the Dana girls and Professor Crandall to be the fugitives whom they had been sent to apprehend.

"It's of no use," Jean said. "They won't believe us."

The situation looked very hopeless indeed. Professor Crandall had been injured in the struggle with the officer, and was too dazed even to try to establish his identity. Harold Norton, the only person who might save them all from the indignity of going to a police station, was in a state of stupor.

"Come along," said one of the men, taking Louise by the arm.

Another pushed Jean toward the door; then halfway across the room he halted abruptly. A strange look came over his face.

"What is it, Joe?"

"Listen!" the officer commanded.

Those in the room could hear an ominous

roar. One of the policemen ran to the door and flung it open. The sound grew louder. It seemed to be a deep rumbling of the mountain itself.

Far above the timber line a cloud of fine dust arose. Stones and sticks began rattling down the slope of the cliff.

"A landslide!" gasped the guard at the door. "Run for your lives!"

The men released the Danas, and rushed over to Warden Norton, whom they dragged from the hermitage.

"Save yourselves!" shouted one of the officers over his shoulder. "This place will be buried in a few minutes!"

Jean and Louise were free at last! They darted over to Professor Crandall, and assisted him to his feet. Feebly he took a step, then crumpled to the floor in a heap.

"It's my leg," he groaned. "It's twisted. I can't walk."

"We'll help you," Jean assured him. "Lean on my arm."

The teacher made a courageous effort to do so, but it was obvious to the girls that he could not walk fast enough, even with their support, to escape the landslide.

The roar had grown louder. Through the open doorway Louise could see that the great avalanche of rock and debris was sliding directly toward the hermitage. In another minute Nina Regan's humble habitation would be buried beneath tons of dirt and rocks.

"Save yourselves," Professor Crandall urged. "You still have time."

Louise and Jean looked at each other. They valued their lives, but they could not desert this man and leave him to a terrible fate.

Louise slammed the door shut. Then she and Jean managed to get the professor into the adjoining cave-like room, which had been hollowed into the cliff and had a rocky structure for a roof.

"This is our only hope," Louise murmured. "Even if the landslide should sweep away the remainder of the hermitage, this part may possibly be spared."

All three of them crouched against the wall, and waited.

The roar became deafening. Boulders and debris pounded overhead. The room was filled with a stifling dust. The trapped group gasped for breath. As if by a miracle, not a stone touched them as they huddled in the shelter.

Within ten minutes the worst was over. Only occasional minor slides occurred following the larger one, but Professor Crandall and the Dana girls did not dare move. After a long wait, during which no further manifestations took place, they decided that it would be safe for them to venture out of their hiding-place. Jean went to the door and opened it, but found herself faced by a solid wall of rock and dirt.

"We're buried alive!" Professor Crandall exclaimed. "This is a tragic end!"

"Let's not give up hope yet," Jean said with forced cheerfulness. "We can perhaps dig our way out."

They all set to work in an effort to move the stones which blocked the exit. Yet, just as they would manage to lift away one of them, there would be another directly back of it. Evidently the outside room, which they had vacated but a few minutes before, had been completely buried.

"It's of no use," Professor Crandall said hopelessly. "We are only deceiving ourselves. Tons of rock must have fallen upon this place."

"Perhaps a rescue party will come before long," Louise ventured optimistically.

The scholarly man shook his head.

"That isn't likely. No one will miss us for several hours. Even then, who would think of looking in such a remote place?"

The Dana girls said nothing. They continued to tug at the stones, but most of them were too heavy to be moved. As Professor Crandall had said, any further effort would be useless.

They were all weak from hunger. Louise glanced at her wrist watch, illuminating it for an instant with a match which Mr. Crandall gave her. It was only eight o'clock, though it seemed as if days had elapsed.

"With night coming on, there's no chance of any help until tomorrow," she said.

"Warden Norton's party may carry word of the catastrophe," Jean ventured.

They all tried to be cheerful, but with the passing of each hour it grew more and more difficult for them to do so. The Dana girls could not forgive themselves for having brought the professor to the hermitage. He, on the other hand, felt that they could have escaped had they not stopped to assist him.

The pitch darkness of the cramped chamber was relieved by a faint gleam of light that came through a tiny aperture high up in the wall. Even had they been able to reach it, they could not have squeezed through the small opening.

After resting, Jean arose, and as she did so, picked up a narrow board she had found in a previous exploration of the inclosure. Thinking that the wall might be hollow, she rapped upon it several times.

"It does have an empty sound," Louise agreed.

Jean tapped again. What was her surprise

to hear a similar sound coming from the other side.

"Did you hear that?" she cried excitedly.

Louise and the professor became alert. The possibility of being rescued appeared to be less remote.

"Try it again," the girl advised tensely.

Jean repeated the knocking, and almost instantly there came answering raps. There could be no question but that some one on the opposite side of the wall knew of their predicament.

"We'll soon be rescued," Jean declared.

From the other side of the partition the tapping had begun again, but this time it seemed to come in dots and dashes.

"A code," Jean commented instantly.

They listened for several minutes, but could not make it out.

"I'm sure it can't be Morse," the professor said. "Why don't they give up their silly tapping and try to get to us?"

Louise spoke quietly. "I doubt that it is a rescue party, Mr. Crandall," she said.

"Then who could it be?"

"Nina Regan. It just occurred to me that she might not have run away after all."

"Instead, she hid herself in a secret room of the hermitage," Jean finished. "Then the child must be with her."

"The situation seems to be growing worse instead of better," Professor Crandall groaned.

"Nina and the child may be trapped in there just as we are here," Jean said. "If we could only talk to her and find out how she is!"

As if in answer to her words, the tapping sounded again. The girls listened closely in an effort to decipher the strange code.

Suddenly an idea came to Jean.

"Why, it's simple!" she cried. "Nina Regan probably learned the trick when she was at Pinecrest."

"You understand the code she's using?" Louise asked eagerly.

Jean strained her ears to make sure that she was right. Then she said:

"It's as simple as the alphabet; in fact, that's what she's using. One tap for A, two for B, and so on. We'll soon be in communication with her!"

So saying, she picked up the board and eagerly set to work, sending out a message of her own.

CHAPTER XVII

RELEASE

In reply to Jean's brief message, the familiar tapping began again. The Dana girls deciphered together the simple alphabetical code.

"It's Nina Regan!" Louise exclaimed.

The message the imprisoned girl sent, when spelled out, was:

"Trapped in secret cave with child. She is hungry and in great pain. Can you help?"

Jean replied immediately, stating briefly the predicament of herself, Louise, and Mr. Crandall. Nina's next message was somewhat longer, and held a note of despair.

"Do not care about rescue for myself. Nothing left in life for me. Please make every effort to save Baby Carol. Do you think she could be squeezed through opening above my head?"

"That might be possible," Professor Crandall admitted. "But we're trapped here, just as Miss Regan is there, so it is hopeless to expect any aid from us."

While Jean was tapping out a reply to Nina,

Louise and Mr. Crandall made another inspection of their prison. They succeeded in locating a loose boulder which had gone by unnoticed. Louise pushed against it with all her strength. To her delight she managed to dislodge it. Then a breath of wind blew against her cheek.

Louise called excitedly to Professor Crandall and her sister and they hurried over to help her.

"I believe we've found a way out!" Jean cried.

For an hour they worked frantically, pushing aside rocks and tearing out loose debris. Louise grew so weary that she had to sit down and rest. Jean, however, kept on doggedly.

Finally an opening large enough to squeeze through was effected. Then the cold night air rushed into their prison. They were saved!

Jean was the first one to crawl through the narrow opening. Professor Crandall finally emerged after the girls had reached safety.

Bewildered, the three looked about them. The first streak of light was coloring the east. Morning would soon come.

"Now let's see if we can get to the child," they cried in one breath.

Jean called out a message to Nina, which was eagerly answered. Then Professor Crandall lifted the girl up until she could reach the tiny opening high in the wall. Carol was then pushed through the narrow aperture.

"I hate to leave Nina behind," Jean murmured. She shouted a message to that effect, and it was instantly answered.

"Don't consider me. Try to get milk for Baby Carol."

"Don't give up hope. We will bring aid," called Jean.

The professor was deeply moved by the Regan girl's display of courage.

"A brave woman," he said as they set out for help. "If we get her away from here alive, I shall do everything in my power to help her to exonerate herself."

As they walked on, the child drew attention to her needs by crying loudly.

"If only we can get some milk!" Jean exclaimed hopefully.

"I wonder if Nina kept a cow," Louise reflected. "I recall her bringing me milk the night I first visited the hermitage."

"I see an animal down by the spring," Professor Crandall said. "Is it a cow?"

"It is!" Jean cried. "Can anyone here milk it?"

"I was reared on a farm," said the professor. "I'll do it."

After the child's hunger had been appeased, the Dana girls and Mr. Crandall had some milk also. Feeling greatly refreshed, they considered ways and means of rescuing Nina.

"We can do nothing by ourselves," the man declared. "First let us take little Carol to a physician and afterward summon aid."

"One of us should stay here," Louise said.

"You might do that," the professor suggested, "while Jean and I go into town."

In order to find the trail to the road, it was necessary for them to retrace their steps to the hermitage. Huge boulders had piled up around its walls, so that only the roof could be seen. Jean, who was in the lead, halted abruptly.

"I believe a rescue party is coming!" she cried.

"Warden Norton's men!" Louise exclaimed in dismay. "They're going to arrest us!"

"Let's hide," Jean urged.

The three secreted themselves with the baby back of the nearest large boulder, where they crouched low, waiting in the hope that the officers would not come by that way. The men drew near the buried cabin and paused to survey the ruins.

"No use looking for them now," one of them said regretfully. "I doubt if they got out alive."

"We barely made it ourselves. They were still in the place when we left," another added. "They're more than likely done for."

Professor Crandall and the worried Dana girls breathed easier. The officers would soon leave.

Baby Carol, who had been asleep in Jean's arms, now opened her eyes and began to cry loudly. The girl tried to quiet the child, but the youngster wailed even more pitifully.

"What's that?" demanded one of the officers sharply.

He walked over to the boulder, where he saw Professor Crandall and the girls hiding.

"So here you are!" he exclaimed. "And I see you have an addition to your party. Tell me, which one of you is Nina Regan?"

No one ventured a reply.

"So you won't talk, eh?" the man demanded irritably. "You'll change your minds later on."

The Dana girls knew that they would not do so. They had no intention of revealing Nina Regan's whereabouts, unless it should become necessary for them to do so to save her life. If they were to tell the officers of the young woman's imprisonment within the hermitage, she doubtless would be rescued, but at the sacrifice of her freedom. Rather would they remain silent for the time being.

Jean and Louise felt confident that as soon as their identity should become known, they would be freed.

In this belief they were correct. They were taken by officers to Clairtown police headquarters where they received an immediate hearing. The judge, who had attended the lecture which the teacher had delivered that afternoon in the auditorium, recognized Professor Crandall at once.

The Dana girls had no difficulty in establishing their own identity after that. The men who had arrested them looked chagrined when Louise stated her reason for going to the hermitage. In telling of her desire to aid the recluse and the crippled child, she carefully avoided giving any sort of clue as to the young woman's whereabouts. Nina was still a fugitive from justice; it was the duty of the officers to arrest her, and the Danas had other plans to carry out.

"What became of this seller of statues?" the judge inquired.

Louise answered truthfully, though evasively.

"When my sister and I went back to look, the situation had changed. The vendor was no longer there."

"Did this person abandon the child when the police got on the trail?"

"I cannot say. After the landslide we found the baby, sick and hungry, in the hermitage."

The judge, who was now convinced that the Dana girls and Professor Crandall were merely the victims of circumstance, dismissed them. The officers who had arrested them realized their mistake as well.

After their release Professor Crandall and the girls took little Carol to a doctor. They were relieved to learn that the child, despite its harrowing experience, was in no immediate danger.

They decided to leave her in the care of a nurse until their return. Then they quietly laid plans for rescuing Nina Regan.

"We must try to save her ourselves," Jean pointed out. "If our moves should become known, the police might take matters into their own hands."

Professor Crandall quietly set about obtaining excavating tools and food. His reluctance to aid Nina Regan was a thing of the past. The young woman's courage had won his admiration so that he was as determined as Louise and Jean that she should be rescued by them.

"We shall have to work swiftly," he told the Dana girls as they unobtrusively left Clairtown to return to the hermitage. "If we cannot reach the woman within a few hours, we shall have to call in the police."

"But only as a last resort," Louise added. "I'm convinced Nina is innocent, and would rather die in the cave than spend any more time at Pinecrest."

...

CHAPTER XVIII

A LAST MESSAGE

WHEN they returned to the hermitage, Professor Crandall and the Dana girls found that
more stones had sealed the cave, and they set
to work in a desperate effort to free the tightly-
imprisoned Nina Regan. One by one they
moved the rocks which barred the entrance.

The heavy work they were doing was decidedly exhausting to Louise and Jean; yet,
when Professor Crandall urged them to rest,
they refused to do so. Their only concern was
for the unfortunate prisoner.

It was nearly noon before the three finally
succeeded in making a hole sufficiently large to
permit a person to crawl through. Since beginning work the Dana girls had heard nothing
from Nina Regan, although they had attempted
several times to communicate with her by
means of tapping signals.

"I fear she is unconscious," Louise said
anxiously, as they peered through the small
opening. "I'm going in and find out."

It was so dark within the cave that at first the
girl could see nothing. As her eyes accustomed

147

themselves to the inky blackness, she saw in a far corner a figure lying inert upon the floor.

"Nina!" she cried, running over.

The young woman stirred slightly and sat up. When she saw Louise, she realized that her rescue would soon be at hand. Springing to her feet, she burst into tears of joy and gratitude.

"I thought you had gone away and left me here alone to die," she sobbed.

"We never would have done that, Nina."

"Is the baby safe?"

"Yes, she is now in the hands of a doctor and a nurse."

"I'm so glad," the young woman murmured brokenly. "After you took the child from me I gave up all hope of ever being saved. It seemed as if hours and hours went by. I must have fallen asleep."

"Here, let me help you out of this dreadful place," Louise said gently. "The opening is barely large enough for you to squeeze through, and be careful not to dislodge any rocks."

With the aid of those outside, Nina escaped from her dungeon. Louise was about to follow her through the opening, when her eyes fell upon a scrap of paper lying on the floor. She felt instinctively that it was a note Nina had written when she believed that death was imminent.

Louise hesitated, then decided to pick up the paper, which she slipped into her pocket.

It was obvious that Nina was suffering from thirst and hunger. While Professor Crandall prepared some food over a camp stove which he had brought along for that purpose, the Dana girls went to a spring for water.

After Nina had had something to eat she endeavored to thank her rescuers for what they had done. It was so difficult for her to speak, however, that they urged her not to try, but to conserve her strength as much as possible. While the sculptress was resting in preparation for the trip back to Clairtown, Louise stole away at the first opportunity to read the note she had found. She was hesitant about perusing it lest Nina, faced with the possibility of death, might have written a confession of the crime of which she had been accused.

"To whom it may concern:" the message began. "I, Nina Regan, knowing that my hours on earth are numbered, wish to reaffirm my innocence in connection with the death of Mrs. Keating and the theft of her jewels.

"It is true the money and jewelry were found in my possession. They were given to me for safekeeping by my employer, who lived in constant fear that she would be robbed. The apprehension was due to the dislike of a distant relative of Mrs. Keating."

The note was left unfinished. Apparently Nina had fallen asleep while composing it. Louise read the message twice before she showed it to her sister. Jean was deeply impressed.

"Surely this proves Nina's innocence, Louise. When she felt that she was about to die, I doubt that she would have written anything but the truth."

"It would seem so. We must do something to help her prove her innocence."

Jean, meanwhile, was re-reading the note.

"I wonder who the distant relative of Mrs. Keating is. If we could find that out, it might provide us with a clue, Louise. This relative may have had Nina convicted through sheer spite."

When the girls returned, they found the young woman greatly improved. She had regained her former poise, and color was coming back into her face. They felt that she would not object to answering a few questions at this time.

Louise led up to the subject tactfully, and to her surprise the sculptress seemed eager to speak of her past. She gave a vivid description of Mrs. Keating, her former employer. The woman was eccentric; though only fifty-five years of age at the time of her death, she was inclined to be childish.

"She believed in hypnotism, and harbored all sorts of superstitious fears," Nina explained. "That was why she wanted me to keep her jewelry for her. She was obsessed with the idea that someone was trying to take it away from her."

"Did you and Mrs. Keating get along well together?" Professor Crandall questioned.

"Oh, yes indeed. Even though she was peculiar, I liked her. Why, I wouldn't have harmed her in any way—to say nothing of doing the terrible thing of which I was accused!"

"Just how did Mrs. Keating meet her death?" asked Jean kindly.

"I only know what I heard later. In some manner the house caught fire while I was away. It stood along the river bank. Even though there was water near by, the structure was almost demolished before the firemen arrived."

"Was Mrs. Keating trapped inside?" Louise prompted.

"Her body was never recovered. One of the men who reached the scene first claimed that he saw Mrs. Keating jump into the river, her clothing ablaze."

"But how could you be convicted on such evidence?" Louise demanded. "Surely it wasn't your fault that the house burned and poor Mrs. Keating was trapped inside."

"No," Nina said wearily, "but the jewels

were found in my possession. I think the case would have been dropped if it hadn't been for a kinsman of Mrs. Keating."

"Can you recall that person's name?" Louise inquired eagerly.

Nina shook her head regretfully.

"No, I cannot. I was so dazed by everything at the time, that the name has left me entirely."

Professor Crandall had been decidedly impressed by the young woman's story. He drew the Dana girls aside to tell them that he would try everything in his power to help the sculptress.

"I may not be doing the right thing," he said, "but even if we act contrary to legal ethics, it would be preferable to sending an innocent person to prison."

"Then will you help us to hide her?" Jean asked eagerly.

"Yes."

"Where can we take her?" Louise questioned, a worried look on her face.

"Why not take her to Mrs. Grantland?" Jean demanded. "I'm sure that kind person will cooperate with us, for she greatly admires Nina Regan's talent."

"We can at least ask her," Louise agreed.

The erstwhile vendor was assisted to Professor Crandall's automobile, and the party started immediately for Penfield. En route, the Regan girl told the Danas about her life at the hermitage.

"How did you ever happen to select such an isolated place?" Jean questioned curiously.

"It was an ideal hide-out. However, I never should have found it had it not been for Baby Carol."

As the girls looked puzzled, she hastened to explain her statement.

"In the reformatory I met a fellow-inmate named Nellie Brice, whose life had been made almost as miserable as my own. We became friendly, and she told me that at the time she was sentenced to Pinecrest she had been forced to leave her baby in the hands of an old nurse, who with her aged husband lived at the hermitage. The man died, and the nurse and little Carol were left penniless. Nellie Brice worried a great deal about the situation.

"At last we decided to try to escape," went on Nina. "We agreed that the one who succeeded in doing so should assume the name Pat Closky, and disguise himself as an old man living at the hermitage."

"You were the one who managed to get away first," Jean commented.

"Yes. I came directly to the isolated abode, where no one would think of looking for me. I found the nurse ill, and unable to care for Babe

Carol properly. I looked after the old lady as long as she lived. Ever since her death I have been staying alone with Nellie's baby.''

"You have been very brave,'' Louise said sincerely. "I feel certain that before many weeks you will be completely exonerated.''

"I shall live in that hope,'' Nina smiled.

The party drove on to Penfield, stopping at Clairtown to get Baby Carol. When they arrived at the home of Mrs. Grantland, the girls told all that had transpired.

"Will you please keep Nina here for a little while?'' Louise pleaded. "She might occupy your third floor for a day or two without anyone growing suspicious. I'm sure she would cause you no trouble.''

Mrs. Grantland was somewhat disturbed at first by the strange request. She hesitated to take a fugitive into her home; yet she could not find it in her heart to turn the sculptress and the child away after she had heard the sad story.

"I really want to be of help,'' the older woman said hastily. "It's only—well, we'll talk it over later. Right now we must make that poor girl comfortable. She looks ill.''

The good lady hurried about, procuring fresh bed linen and preparing the third floor for occupancy. Nina was so exhausted by the harrowing events of the past few hours that she fell asleep almost as soon as her head touched the pillow.

Professor Crandall and Mrs. Grantland later discussed what they considered the best plan. They could arrive at no decision, however, and concluded that it would be better to wait until Mr. Grantland and Mrs. Crandall should join in the conference.

"It looks as if we're to be deprived of any further work on this case," Jean commented ruefully to her sister as they were returning to Starhurst. "That's one thing I don't like about older persons. They're always too willing to take matters out of young people's hands!"

"We found Nina, and we should really have some voice in the affair," Louise added feelingly.

They felt considerably better about things the next day when they were asked to come to Mrs. Grantland's home for a conference. Professor and Mrs. Crandall and Mr. Grantland were also present.

"I think we ought to keep Nina under cover until we get absolute proof of her innocence," Louise argued.

Jean concurred in her sister's opinion. The older people listened politely, but it was obvious that they were not convinced of the wisdom of such a plan.

"I think the authorities will grant Nina a parole when they hear her story," Professor Crandall maintained. "I propose that we place the case before them without delay."

"And hire a good lawyer to re-open the case," Mrs. Grantland added.

Louise and Jean protested that they were afraid the reformatory officials and the board of parole would not look at the matter in the same light. In the end they were overruled by their elders. It was decided that Mr. and Mrs. Grantland, together with Professor and Mrs. Crandall, should make the trip to Pinecrest Reformatory to intercede in the Regan girl's behalf.

"And Louise and Jean shall stay here and look after Nina," Mrs. Grantland said hastily, noting their downcast faces. "You're to have complete charge of the house until we return."

The girls accepted their lot with good grace. However, after the older people had started for Pinecrest, Jean and Louise dejectedly climbed the stairs to Nina Regan's quarters.

"No use in our telling her where everyone has gone," Jean warned. "Of course, there's a chance they'll bring back good news, though I doubt it."

"So do I," added Louise in a discouraged tone. "I have a feeling that Nina Regan's troubles are only just beginning."

CHAPTER XIX

BAD NEWS

NINA REGAN was busy with some sewing when the Dana girls entered the cozy room on the third floor. She greeted them with a gay smile which belied her recent experiences.

"I see you've found work for yourself," Louise said cheerfully.

"Yes, I'm making a little dress for Carol. She's almost outgrown her others. Mrs. Grantland gave me the material."

The smile faded from Nina's face for an instant as her dark eyes rested upon the deformed child lying on a bed.

"Carol appears stronger to me," she said in a half-whisper, "and yet, I wonder——"

"I think the baby is gaining strength every day," Jean declared. "Perhaps she'll soon be able to walk."

"I'd give anything in the world if that could only happen! But I haven't even money enough to call in a specialist to examine her."

Louise and Jean were happy that they could provide a bit of cheering news. The latter said:

157

"Mrs. Grantland was talking about little Carol today. She wants to look after her and see that she has the medical attention she needs."

A beautiful light shone in Nina's eyes.

"How good of her! Oh, everyone has been so kind to me!"

"You deserve it," Louise smiled. "It shouldn't be long now until you will be cleared of the old charge against you. Then you can pick up the threads of your life and begin anew."

"I owe everything to you and Jean," Nina declared gratefully. Then she abruptly changed the subject. "I've finished Carol's dress. Isn't there some sewing I can do for you girls?"

They shook their heads; but Nina's keen eye had noticed a torn hem in Louise's dress, which she insisted upon mending.

"You sew beautifully," Louise praised.

"I've always been able to do things with my hands. I enjoy it, too. I even like to set hair and manicure nails."

"I might give you a job working on me," Jean laughed. "My hair is a sight."

She had not intended the remark to be taken seriously, but Nina had soon found a comb and some bobby pins. Jean's short bob was soon transformed into a mass of curly ringlets.

"I used to spend a lot of time on my appearance," Nina confessed, as she worked. "Of course, now I am no longer young or attractive."

"You mustn't say that," Jean reproved. "Your face has lots of character."

"You're still beautiful," Louise added.

"I wonder if Fred Lester would think so," Nina murmured, not realizing that she had spoken aloud.

Jean and Louise looked up quickly. Nina had never mentioned that name before.

"Were you and he old friends?" the latter asked with interest.

"More than that. We were engaged to be married at the time of my conviction. Of course, I returned his ring to him."

"But wouldn't he have waited for you?"

"I couldn't have permitted such a sacrifice. It would have ruined Lester's career."

"You must have loved him deeply to have been able to give him up," Jean said softly.

"I did," returned Nina, and changed the subject.

She began to talk of her former employer and the peculiar friends Mrs. Keating had so often brought to her home.

"There was one woman in particular," she related. "Mrs. X.Y.Z., everyone called her. She had a powerful influence over my employer. I've often wondered whatever became of her."

"Have you seen her since the fire?" Louise inquired.

"No, she disappeared completely."

"Didn't you ever hear her real name?"

"I doubt that I have ever heard it. Mrs. Keating always spoke of her friend as Mrs. X.Y.Z."

"A strange appellation," Jean laughed.

"Yes, and she was a strange person, too."

"It's a pity you can't recall the names of any of Mrs. Keating's close friends or relatives," Louise said thoughtfully.

Jean threw her sister a quick glance. It was clear to her that Louise was afraid Nina might have difficulty in proving her innocence. Yet why did she believe that the missing kinsman might shed some light upon the subject? Secretly Jean was disappointed. It seemed to her that the mystery surrounding Mrs. Keating's death was as deep as ever.

When the two girls were alone for a few minutes, she voiced a similar thought to Louise.

"Yes," her sister admitted, "as far as we're concerned, Nina has already proven her innocence. But to make the parole board believe that might be an entirely different matter. It's queer that no trace of Mrs. Keating's body was ever found."

Although the Dana girls had appeared cheerful in Nina's presence, they were far from being optimistic about the young woman's future. Louise in particular felt depressed. For some reason which she could not explain, she sensed impending trouble.

The roar of an automobile drew the Dana girls to the window. Mr. and Mrs. Grantland and the Crandalls were returning from Pinecrest.

Louise and Jean ran out to meet them.

"Any luck?" the latter called.

One glance at the discouraged faces of the four adults told the story. They had failed.

Prepared as they were for an unfavorable report, Jean and Louise were greatly disheartened when they learned the outcome of the trip.

"We did the best we could, but it was futile," Mrs. Grantland explained sadly. "Nina must go back to Pinecrest."

"But surely not for long?" Louise cried.

"I am afraid it will be for many years," Mrs. Crandall told the girls reluctantly. "Her sentence may be extended because of her attempted escape, and she is to be placed in solitary confinement as well."

"Oh, how cruel!" Jean exclaimed.

"We did everything we could, and we'll use every means in our power to get the decision reversed," Professor Crandall said. "We have already engaged a lawyer for her."

"I shall take care of the child," Mrs. Grantland added. "Baby Carol shall be taken to the best orthopedic specialist in the state."

"How can we break the news to Nina about her sentence?" Louise asked. "It may kill her."

Mrs. Grantland was elected to deliver the verdict to the young woman. Nina accepted it more calmly than anyone had expected her to.

"When must I leave?" she questioned, brushing tears from her eyes.

"This evening, I am afraid, my dear. The officials are sending an officer to take you."

"So soon?"

Nina's anguished eyes sought the sympathetic ones of the older woman; then they roved to the window. The last rays of the setting sun were shining through the panes.

"I have given my word that you will not try to escape," Mrs. Grantland said.

"No, I'll stay. I am tired of hiding. This time I shall accept my fate. But it is very disheartening."

"Don't lose courage, my dear. You now have friends who will do everything in their power to help you."

"Everyone has been so good," Nina sobbed. "So good."

Jean and Louise came up presently to bid Nina good-bye, for they had decided not to wait until the arrival of the official from Pine-crest. They felt that to see the sculptress actually being taken away would be more than they could stand without protesting vigorously.

"I'll never forget your kindness to me and to little Carol," Nina told them. "And perhaps some day you'll come to see me."

"We surely will," Jean said, her voice breaking. "But you won't be gone very long!"

"We'll find a way to prove your innocence," Louise added, holding the young woman's hand. "Keep up your courage until you hear from us."

The Dana girls left the house a few minutes later, deciding to walk to Starhurst. After they had gone a block they looked back, and could see the prison automobile driving up to the door. Then they hurriedly walked on.

"If they keep her there, I must say there's absolutely no justice in this world!" Jean muttered.

"She was so brave," Louise added dejectedly.

Walking along slowly, their heads bent low, they failed to see a man who was approaching from the opposite direction until they ran directly into him.

"Warden Norton!" Louise exclaimed, startled.

He chuckled in delight.

"I'm not after you this time, Miss Dana. We've got the real Nina Regan at last!"

Jean glared at him, a look of deep disgust on her face.

"I guess Nina will never get away again," Norton went on in fiendish glee. "We're putting her in a good safe place this time."

"You seem to be terribly thrilled over her misfortune," Louise said coldly.

"Why shouldn't I be? She's a criminal of the worst type."

"That hasn't been proven to the satisfaction of most people!" Louise retorted.

"Some things don't have to be proven," the ex-warden chuckled slyly.

He turned as if to walk on; then Jean, infuriated by his attitude, whirled upon him. She had been goaded beyond her endurance.

"I believe you know more about this case than you care to admit!" she said sharply.

"And so does Mrs. X.Y.Z.," Louise cried, catching the man by the arm.

"I—I don't know what you're talking about," the man stammered.

But all the color had drained from his face, and he looked as if he might faint.

CHAPTER XX

The Mysterious Mrs. X.Y.Z.

"You *do* know something about it!" Louise cried triumphantly.

Ex-Warden Norton jerked his arm free, and before the Dana girls could prevent him, he had rushed away. By the time he reached the corner he was actually running.

"We certainly frightened him that time," Jean declared excitedly. "Did you see the look on his face when we accused him of knowing more about the case than he cared to tell?"

"I should say I did. And when I mentioned Mrs. X.Y.Z. I thought he would faint! Jean, he must know that woman."

"He ran away because he was afraid to answer our questions. Oh, Louise, I believe we've struck a valuable clue."

"I feel certain of it. Norton is hiding something, that's evident."

"He has a secret motive for wanting Nina Regan put in jail," Jean added. "Oh, if we could only find out what it is!"

"The thing for us to do is to locate this mysterious Mrs. X.Y.Z."

165

"But how can we do that when we don't even know her real name?"

"Perhaps we can think of some way of tracing her if we put our minds to it," Louise declared.

They did very little studying that day at school. However, their instructors were lenient, having learned from Mrs. Crandall of the Dana girls' distressing experience in regard to Nina Regan. Though Louise and Jean cudgeled their brains, they could think of no way of locating the missing Mrs. X.Y.Z.

They were still considering the problem that evening, when Jean, glancing up from her book, casually mentioned that the *Balaska* had docked in New York the day before.

"Then Uncle Ned must be at home," Louise said. "I hope he comes to see us, and brings Aunt Harriet with him."

"I doubt if he'll be able to get over to Starhurst this time. The *Balaska* sails again in a few days."

"I almost wish I were going along," Louise sighed. "Uncle Ned has such wonderful experiences and meets such fascinating people."

"I wonder if Mrs. X.Y.Z. has ever traveled on his boat?" Jean mused, half in jest.

Louise sprang to her feet.

"Now that's an idea! Why didn't you think of it before?"

"Where are you going?" Jean demanded, as Louise started for the door.

"To telephone Uncle Ned," Louise replied.

"Why do that?"

"When you mentioned Mrs. X.Y.Z. in connection with Uncle Ned, I suddenly recalled that he once spoke of a peculiar passenger who sailed on his ship last year."

"Uncle Ned has plenty of queer voyagers."

"Of course. But I seem to recall that he spoke of this person as a Mrs. X.Y.Z. I may be mistaken, however."

"You probably are."

"Well, it won't do any harm to find out."

The telephones were at the end of the hall. Louise waited until the booths were empty, for she did not want her conversation to be overheard by anyone. She called Oak Falls, and presently Aunt Harriet's pleasing voice came from the other end of the wire.

After chatting for a few minutes, and assuring her relative that nothing serious was the matter, Louise asked to speak to Uncle Ned. She half expected that he would laugh when he heard why she had phoned him, but he listened attentively to her request for information about Mrs. X.Y.Z.

"Seems to me I once did have a woman aboard my ship who used the alphabet instead of a name," he said. "Shiver my topsails!

What was her right name anyway?'' he said, wrinkling his forehead in an effort to remember it.

Louise waited with bated breath, saying nothing.

"I seem to recollect an odd sort of woman on my ship a long time ago—a Mrs. Xenia Young Zellow. Could that have been the one you've in mind?''

"It might be the person I'm looking for, Uncle Ned. Can you tell me where she lives?''

"I couldn't do that offhand, my dear. I'd have to look up the old passenger list files.''

"Would that be inconvenient for you?''

"Not for an old sea dog like your Uncle Ned. Be glad to do it. Now just keep your ballast for a couple of days until I can get all the facts.''

Louise chatted a few minutes longer, then hung up the receiver and hurried back to tell Jean the exciting news.

"Oh, I hope Uncle Ned finds her address!'' Jean exclaimed, putting down her French book with gusto. "I'm so thrilled I can't study another minute.''

"Another, did you say?'' Louise jested. "If I'm any judge, you haven't studied a minute all day.''

In truth, both girls were so wrought up over the events of the past two days that they did not sleep well that night. They awoke earlier than usual to see the morning sun streaming in through their windows.

Jean yawned, then surprised her sister by jumping out of bed.

"Up already?"

"Might as well. I can't sleep."

"But no one else is up. The breakfast gong won't sound for fully two hours yet."

Jean had gone to the window, and was looking down upon the courtyard.

"You're mistaken about no one being up," she announced.

"The milkman?"

"No, Lettie Briggs."

"Lettie!" Louise bounded out of bed to join her sister at the window. "Why, she's the laziest person in the dormitory. What aroused her so early, I wonder?"

"She's carrying a bundle, too. Wouldn't you love to know where she's going?"

"I can dress in five minutes," Louise laughed.

"Make it three," Jean challenged, snatching her stockings from the foot of the bed.

They were downstairs before Lettie had disappeared from sight. She was walking slowly in the direction of the gardener's cottage. Unaware that she was being watched by the Danas, the girl sought the man who tended the school grounds, and handed the bundle to him quickly.

"Thank you so much for lending me the clothes," Louise and Jean heard her say.

"You were pretty slow in returning them," the gardener replied.

"The masquerade party wasn't held quite as early as I thought it would be," Lettie said hastily.

At this point in the conversation the Dana girls sauntered up to the cottage. Lettie grew flustered when she saw them, and was curious to know how much they had heard and seen.

"Did I hear you say something about a masquerade party?" Jean inquired pointedly.

"Why, yes," Lettie stammered.

"Was there a masquerade at Starhurst?" Louise inquired mischievously. "I didn't hear of one."

"That was several days ago," the gardener said sincerely. "Another girl came to see me about getting a suit of clothes, too."

"That must have been Ina," Jean surmised. She bent down and deliberately tore a small hole in the bundle. "Do you recognize these garments, Louise?"

"Yes, I do."

Her eyes met those of Lettie. The latter had the grace to look ashamed, however, knowing that the Dana girls were aware of the trick she had played at the river.

"You were the one who masqueraded as Warden Norton," Louise said quietly.

"Well, what of it? It was only a joke. I didn't mean any harm by it." Angrily she turned and hurried back to the dormitory.

Before the day had ended several students had heard of the girl's cruelty in abandoning the unconscious Louise at the waterfall. Lettie was ostracized by everyone except Ina.

"We ought to tell Mrs. Crandall the whole story," Doris Harland insisted when the tale reached her ears. "I'm sure she'd have Lettie expelled if she were to learn about it."

Louise would not permit the story to be carried further, however, feeling that the Briggs girl was being punished sufficiently.

Late that evening the Dana girls received a brief wire from Captain Dana.

"Mrs. X.Y.Z. (Xenia Young Zellow) resides at Crow's Point," it read. "This may be woman you mean."

"Oh, I'm sure it is!" Jean cried in delight. "Where is Crow's Point?"

They took down an atlas, and eagerly pored over a map of their state. The place was not far from Penfield. "We could make it over a week-end," Louise declared enthusiastically.

"You mean we might if Mrs. Crandall would permit us to go. She's very much opposed to week-end trips."

"Maybe Mrs. Grantland will accompany us. That would surely be all right with Mrs. Crandall."

At their first opportunity the girls hastened to Penfield to see Mrs. Grantland. When the good woman learned that the trip might benefit Nina Regan, she readily consented to chaperon them.

"Have you heard from Nina since we last saw you?" Jean inquired.

"No, the officers took her away shortly after you left. The lawyer we hired is doing everything in his power to re-open the case, but thus far hasn't been very successful. He says we need additional evidence."

"And that's what I hope the trip to Crow's Point will yield," Louise said.

The Dana girls were told that Baby Carol had been taken to a hospital that specialized in the care of crippled children.

"I think the child would progress more rapidly if she could see Nina," Mrs. Grantland said hopefully. "The poor little thing thinks the young woman is her mother."

Louise and Jean awaited impatiently the arrival of Saturday. Never had a week seemed so long to them. However, the last class on Friday finally came to an end, and they were free to pack their bags for the anticipated trip to Crow's Point.

Mrs. Grantland called at the school for the girls, announcing that she wanted to go back to her home before leaving Penfield. Jean and Louise waited outside, and a few minutes later were surprised to see the woman hurrying toward them, her face drawn into worried lines.

"I've just received word from the Children's Hospital," she told the girls.

"The baby isn't ill, is she?" Jean asked anxiously.

"Seriously so, I'm afraid. The doctors are worried for fear she will not live. They want me to bring her mother to her at once."

"Her mother," Louise echoed. "You mean her real mother—Nellie Brice? But how can we when she's at Pinecrest?"

"I said I'd do my best to get in touch with her."

"We shall have to give up the trip to Crow's Point and drive at once to Pinecrest," Jean cried. "There's a possibility that the officials will let Nellie go to the hospital to see her child."

"At least for a few hours," Louise added.

"We'll find out," Mrs. Grantland decided. "I only hope we'll not be too late."

The trip to the reformatory was made at break-neck speed. However, for the second time Mrs. Grantland and the Dana girls were to find themselves baffled by the strict laws of the institution. Mrs. Selzer listened sympathetically to their story, but when they had finished she merely shook her head.

"Nellie Brice has never been a model prisoner. For months she has been awaiting an opportunity to escape."

"But what can that have to do with the present situation?" Mrs. Grantland cried. "Her baby is dying."

"I am sorry, but we can't let her go. She might try to make a getaway."

"Is there nothing we can do or say to make you change your decision?"

"Nothing. I only wish I might grant your request."

Completely discouraged, Mrs. Grantland and the Dana girls filed out of the office and returned to the waiting automobile.

CHAPTER XXI

At Crow's Point

Leaving Pinecrest Reformatory behind them, Mrs. Grantland and the Dana girls sped to the Children's Hospital, where they spoke to one of the nurses.

"Baby Carol Brice has rallied," she told the visitors. "At present she is out of danger."

"I'm so happy to hear it," Mrs. Grantland said in relief. "May we see the child?"

"Visitors might excite and tire her, so she must see no one today. She calls constantly for 'Nina.' If it were possible for that person, or perhaps the child's mother, to come——"

"It's futile," Mrs. Grantland sighed. "We have done all we can, and it is of no use to try further."

Ten minutes later they left the hospital, somewhat assured with the thought that for the time being little Carol was in no danger of a relapse. Mrs. Grantland's generosity had provided the child with every necessity, and nurses were in constant attendance.

"What shall we do now?" the woman asked,

as the three returned to the car. "Shall we continue on to Crow's Point?"

Jean and Louise eagerly assented. They could not help Baby Carol by remaining at the hospital, while at Crow's Point they might glean valuable information which would free Nina Regan.

Mrs. Grantland did not share the Dana girls' enthusiasm for the trip, though she was perfectly willing to accompany them. She felt certain that the mysterious Mrs. X.Y.Z. had no connection whatsoever with Nina Regan's case, yet she refrained from discouraging her friends by suggesting such a thought.

Before they had driven very far, they noticed that the gasoline gauge registered low, so they began to watch for a filling station. Presently Louise called attention to one directly ahead, and they drove in.

A pleasant-faced young man came running out to serve them. Louise stared first at him, then at the sign above the little office, which read: "Fred Lester, Proprietor."

"Are you Mr. Fred Lester, the owner of this place?" she questioned at the first opportunity. It was quite possible that he might be only an employee.

"Yes, I am Fred Lester," the young man smiled. "I bought the station only a few months ago. Times have been hard, but recently I've been making a little money. I can surely use it, too.''

"You may as well fill up the tank," said Mrs. Grantland. She had intended to buy only five gallons, but the young man's personality appealed to her and she wanted to help him.

On the pretext of getting a little exercise, Jean and Louise stepped from the car and walked around to the rear, where they watched the proprietor efficiently manipulate the gasoline pump. They scrutinized his face carefully, and judged him to be a little over thirty years of age. Could he by any chance be the Fred Lester whom Nina had known?

"Ask him," Jean whispered.

Louise hesitated, for the subject was a delicate one. Finally she ventured to inquire if he had ever known a girl named Nina Regan. Fred Lester almost dropped the gasoline hose. He looked sharply at the girls, but could see only sympathy and interest in their eyes.

"Yes, I knew her well," he answered quietly. "Are you her friends?"

Louise assured him that they were. She then related a little of what had transpired during the past week, stating that she and her sister were on their way to Crow's Point in the hope of securing evidence which might free Nina.

"I never thought she was guilty," Fred

Lester declared earnestly. "We broke off our engagement only because she would not have it otherwise."

"You still love her, don't you?" Jean asked softly.

"Yes, but I feel that I have failed her."

"In what way?" Louise inquired.

"I haven't been able to help her clear herself. It costs money to hire lawyers, and until the past few months I haven't earned hardly anything."

"I am sure Nina understands," Jean said.

"I'm studying law at night whenever I'm not working here," the young man stated. "I don't know why I tell you all these things—you can't possibly be interested."

"Oh, but we are!" Louise declared quickly. "And you mustn't feel greatly discouraged about Nina's future, either. I think that before many weeks will have elapsed, we shall have evidence which will result in her release."

"I'll do anything in my power to help," Fred Lester said eagerly.

The Dana girls presented him to Mrs. Grantland; then they chatted pleasantly until another car drove in for gasoline.

"We must be on our way," the lady declared reluctantly. "But we'll surely drop in again on our return trip."

Mrs. Grantland and the friendly Dana girls

had started later than they had intended from
Penfield, so that it was almost dark by the
time they reached Crow's Point. After securing lodgings for themselves at a hotel, they
learned from the clerk that Mrs. Xenia Young
Zellow's cottage was located on the far tip of
Crow's Point.

"I doubt if you'll find her at home now,"
the attendant told them. "Mrs. Zellow spends
most of her time traveling. It seems to me
someone said she is now away."

Mrs. Grantland was exhausted after the long
day's drive. The thought of going to Mrs.
Zellow's cottage and not finding the woman
at home, did not appeal to her.

"If you don't mind, I'll stay here at the
hotel," she announced, "while you girls take
the car. You won't need me, anyway."

After dinner Louise and Jean set off alone
for the Point. The road wound in and out
along the shore, the houses being few and far
between. The girls stopped once to ask the
way to the Zellow cottage, and were told it
was the last house on the road.

"I don't suppose we'll find the woman at
home," Louise said in a discouraged tone.
"I'm sure Mrs. Grantland thinks the trip has
been in vain."

"She's a wonderful sport to take us wher-
ever we want to go," Jean added.

They drew up near the cottage and parked the car. Both girls were disappointed to find the place in darkness.

"I guess the hotel clerk was right," Jean said. "The house is deserted."

They were on the point of turning back without even going to the door, when they saw two middle-aged women coming up the walk. Each of them carried a suitcase, and they were laughing and talking animatedly.

"Who can that be?" Jean whispered.

"Let's wait and find out where they go."

The strangers hurried up to the front entrance of the cottage. One of them took a key from her purse and unlocked the door, and the two walked in.

"Do you think Mrs. Zellow has just returned from a trip?" Jean asked.

The lights were suddenly turned on inside the bungalow, and the girls observed the women removing their wraps.

"Let's see what we can find out," Jean proposed.

They left the car, and quietly made their way to the front porch.

"Open the window, Henriette," one of the women directed in a voice audible to the Dana girls. "It is so stuffy in here."

"Yes, Xenia," the other said, hastening to obey.

In the darkness Jean and Louise gripped each other's hands. Their quest had *not* been in vain. Xenia Young Zellow—the mysterious Mrs. X.Y.Z., had returned home!

"I declare, Henriette, I feel years younger than I did when I went away," she said.

"So do I, my dear," her companion added, laughing gaily. "The trip did wonders for both of us. I feel now as if I could cope with any situation that might arise."

"You mean——"

"Oh, nothing at all, my dear. I was merely rambling."

Jean and Louise were fairly overcome with curiosity. They could not imagine who Mrs. X.Y.Z.'s friend might be. Certainly they were unprepared for the next startling revelation. Mrs. Zellow's remark, short and apparently insignificant, gave them the clue to the entire situation.

"Henriette Keating," she said joyfully, "isn't it nice to be back home? I doubt if I shall ever care to travel again."

Jean and Louise were aghast. Had their ears deceived them? Mrs. Keating! According to all reports, she had perished in the fire.

"There must have been some dreadful mistake," Jean whispered.

Louise nodded. "We have all the evidence we need, Jean. Nina Regan is absolved!"

CHAPTER XXII

A Deserted House

LOUISE and Jean were so thrilled over this important disclosure that they rushed to the front door of the cottage and rang the bell. Mrs. Zellow answered their summons.

"You are Mrs. Zellow, are you not?" Jean began eagerly.

With a look of surprise, the woman acknowledged her identity. "Do you wish to see me?" she asked.

"Yes. My sister and I journeyed all the way from Penfield hoping to find you here. May we come in?"

Mrs. Zellow frowned slightly. It was not to her liking to have guests so soon after her arrival.

"Everything in the house is upset," she apologized. "I returned from a trip only a few minutes ago."

"We wouldn't bother you at this time of night, only it's most important," Louise urged.

"Very well. Come in."

As the Dana girls entered the living room, Mrs. Keating looked sharply at them. She half arose as if to leave, then apparently changed her mind.

Louise and Jean waited expectantly, hoping that Mrs. Zellow would introduce her companion, but she made no move to do so.

"We came here thinking that you might help us locate your friend Mrs. Keating," Louise said significantly.

The two women stared at each other, and then as quickly looked away.

"My dear girl," Mrs. Zellow said after a moment's deliberation, "I can't imagine why you should come here looking for Mrs. Keating. Have you not heard of the disastrous fire which destroyed her home? She disappeared at the time, and it is believed that she perished in the flames."

"We are familiar with the story," Louise said dryly. "That's one reason why we came to you. Surely you can tell us what really happened to her."

Again the two women exchanged questioning glances. The Dana girls distinctly saw Mrs. Keating signal her friend that her true identity was not to be revealed.

"I am afraid I can't tell you anything," Mrs. Zellow said pleasantly. "The affair is closed, and I see no reason for opening it again."

Such an attitude was too much for the Dana girls to bear. Impulsively Jean burst out:

"The case isn't closed, and it never can be until Nina Regan is freed!"

"What has she to do with it?" Mrs. Keating asked, speaking for the first time.

"She was sentenced to imprisonment at Pinecrest," Louise stated. "She was convicted of robbing her employer, Mrs. Keating, and of being responsible for her death."

"Oh," Mrs. Keating murmured. "I never knew that!"

The Dana girls decided that it was time for them to explain everything.

"Why don't you end this pretense?" Jean said abruptly. "You will save yourself a great deal of trouble if you will tell us you are Mrs. Keating."

The woman looked deeply troubled, but remained silent.

"You may have some reason for not wishing to be known," Jean went on, "but please think of poor Nina. Her life has been ruined."

"You have it in your power to free her from prison," Louise added.

Mrs. Keating arose from the couch. She paced up and down the room twice, then turned and faced the girls.

"Very well, I will admit that I am Mrs. Keating. I had no idea that Nina Regan would be accused of burning the house when I planned to run off the way I did."

"Then you knew of the fire at the time?"

"Knew of it? Of course I did. I set fire to the place myself."

Had a bomb exploded in the room, Louise and Jean could not have been more astounded. Nina Regan was now completely absolved of all guilt.

"The house was mine," Mrs. Keating said crossly in her own defense. "And if I wanted to burn it down it seems to me that was my own business, too."

"That's true," Louise acknowledged, "but when an innocent person is blamed——"

"I didn't intend to make trouble for Nina Regan," Mrs. Keating interrupted. "It never occurred to me that anyone would accuse her of setting fire to my home."

"Why did you do it?" Jean asked.

"Because I wanted to," Mrs. Keating snapped. "I was sick and tired of that old house, anyway. A regular old barn, it was. Hard to keep clean, and expensive to heat."

"But that wasn't your *real* reason for burning it," Louise probed.

"Well, maybe it wasn't. But if you're thinking I did it to collect any insurance money you're wrong. I had some personal troubles of my own which I won't go into. A distant relative of mine—I'll not mention his name—caused me considerable annoyance."

"It was worse than that," Mrs. Zellow interposed.

"Yes, this relative exercised a strange power over me. I was afraid of him, and of what he might do. In desperation I set fire to my house, and let it appear that I had been burned to death in it."

"And then where did you go?" Jean inquired, as Mrs. Keating paused in her narrative.

"To Africa with my friend, Mrs. X.Y.Z. We had a glorious time too, didn't we, Xenia?"

"Marvelous!"

"I put my old life behind me," the woman went on. Then her tone abruptly changed, and she smiled at the Dana girls as she added, "I know you think me a peculiar old lady. Perhaps I am. But at my age it seems that I should have the privilege of spending the rest of my days as I see fit."

"Of course you have, as long as your doing so doesn't cause trouble for other people," Louise agreed.

"I don't see why Nina Regan was ever accused of the crime."

"Your jewelry was found in her possession."

"I gave those to her for safe-keeping. In my hurry to get out of this country I forgot all about them."

"I doubt that Nina would have been accused

if it hadn't been for Ex-Warden Norton," Jean remarked. "He pushed the case against her."

"Norton?" Mrs. Keating gasped. "You mean Harold Norton?"

Before either of the Dana girls could say anything, the woman had slumped back onto the sofa. Her face grew pale, and she looked as if she were going to faint.

"My heart," she murmured weakly.

Louise and Jean hurried to assist the victim, but Mrs. Zellow turned upon them in sudden anger.

"Don't you dare touch her!" she fairly screamed. "You're responsible for her condition. You came here and upset her. Leave my house this instant."

"Please, Mrs. Zellow—" Jean began.

The woman cut her short. "Go at once, or I shall call the police and have you put out!"

Louise and Jean had no alternative but to leave. When they were once outside the cottage, they held an animated discussion.

"We have all the evidence we need, Jean."

"Yes, but we should have had witnesses to Mrs. Keating's story."

"Let's go back to the hotel and get Mrs. Grantland."

"All right. But will Mrs. Zellow let us in the house again?"

"We'll find some way to manage it. Mrs.

Grantland will help, I feel sure. She's wonderfully diplomatic at handling difficult people.''

"Mrs. Keating and Mrs. X.Y.Z. surely are a strange pair,'' Louise chuckled, as the sisters hurried over to the parked car. "I wonder why they both were so stunned when we mentioned Norton's name?''

"There are a number of mysterious angles to the case, Louise. Mrs. Keating really didn't explain matters at all clearly. She had some sinister motive in burning that house—and she hasn't revealed it, either!''

"We'll speak to her again. Perhaps next time we'll learn more.''

Mrs. Grantland was preparing to retire for the night when the girls reached her room at the hotel. When she learned of the evidence they had uncovered, she became almost as excited as the two Danas.

"Jean and Louise, you have accomplished a marvelous piece of detective work,'' she praised. "What a blessing it will be for poor Nina Regan, when it is made known that she really is innocent.''

"If Mrs. Keating would go to the authorities and tell them the truth, I know Nina would be freed,'' Louise declared happily. "You'll talk to the woman and her friend, won't you?''

"Of course. I'll do all in my power to try

to make them see things reasonably. However, I think we should wait until morning to do that.''

"I guess that would be better," Jean agreed somewhat reluctantly. "Both women were naturally tired and upset from their trip. When we left the cottage Mrs. Keating was in no condition to speak to anyone."

"She'll doubtless feel more rested in the morning," Mrs. Grantland smiled. "Frankly, I feel confident we can handle her all right."

Shortly after breakfast the following morning the little party left for the cottage on Crow's Point.

"The house looks to be boarded up," Mrs. Grantland observed as they drew near.

"I suppose they haven't had time to unpack things yet," Louise remarked.

They parked the automobile and went up the walk. All the windows were tightly closed. For the first time the Dana girls experienced an uneasy sensation.

Mrs. Grantland rang the doorbell several times, but no one answered it. In the meantime, the Dana girls had gone around to the back door. They even peered into a window, but everything looked deserted.

Gradually the truth began to dawn upon them—Mrs. Keating and her friend had fled!

CHAPTER XXIII

ABSOLVED

KEENLY disappointed over their failure to
find Mrs. Keating, the Dana girls and Mrs.
Grantland returned to their hotel. They were
convinced now that the woman, frightened by
so much questioning, had gone into hiding.

"We'll never find her," Jean said in dis-
couragement. "For some reason she is afraid
to tell her story to the authorities."

"I suppose we may as well drive back to
Penfield," Mrs. Grantland sighed. "Probably
the best thing for us to do would be to turn
the case over to a private detective agency.
They may be able to trace the woman."

Louise said nothing. If Mrs. Keating were
not located within the next few hours, she
doubted that anyone would ever succeed in
finding her. More than likely she and Mrs.
Zellow would sail for some far distant port,
perhaps to make their home in a foreign land.

"I think I'll go to church while you girls are
packing," Mrs. Grantland said presently. "I
noticed a church just a short distance from the
hotel."

No sooner had Mrs. Grantland departed, than Louise began throwing garments into her suitcase with little regard for the manner in which they were packed.

"Why the rush?" Jean demanded.

"Because we have some very important things to do. I have a hunch Mrs. Keating is still in this town, and I intend to find her!"

"That's easier said than done."

"It was late in the evening when we saw the two women," Louise ruminated. "Is it likely that they would leave Crow's Point before morning?"

"No, it isn't, but where can they have gone?"

"Why not to this hotel?" Louise demanded.

"I didn't think of that. They might be here. Let's look at the register."

Leaving their packing for the moment, they went down to the lobby and asked the clerk to show them the list of recent arrivals. Two women had registered the previous night, but their names were unfamiliar to the Dana girls.

"Looks as if your idea were wrong, Louise."

"It's possible they used assumed names," Louise maintained. "We must try to find out more about these two people."

The clerk at the desk, a different one from the man they had asked information of the evening before, would tell the girls nothing, save that they were elderly women who desired the strictest privacy. Jean had noticed that the number of their room was listed as 309.

"We may as well go up there now and talk to them," she suggested to her sister after they were out of earshot of the man.

As they alighted from the elevator, a boy carrying an empty breakfast tray emerged from a room at the end of the hall. Jean's keen eyes noted that it was number 309. She halted the attendant as he passed, and adroitly questioned him concerning the identity of the women he had just served.

"I don't know their names," he returned indifferently. "One called the other Xenia."

Jean and Louise were elated at the information. As soon as the boy had disappeared down the stairs, they rapped upon the door.

"Come in," said a familiar voice.

They entered, to find Mrs. Zellow and Mrs. Keating seated near a window. At sight of the Dana girls they started to their feet.

"You have followed me here!" Mrs. Keating cried fearfully. "Oh! What shall I do?"

"Don't get excited," Louise said quickly. "We shall make no trouble for you. Our only object is to help Nina Regan."

For an instant it appeared as if Mrs. Keating were on the verge of another attack of nerves. However, she controlled herself and sank back in her chair.

"Please go!" Mrs. Zellow cried. "Can't you see that you are exciting my friend?"

"Let them stay," Mrs. Keating said unexpectedly. "They may as well know the truth. Then I can have a clear conscience once more."

For a moment the woman leaned against the pillows, her eyes closed. She appeared to be summoning courage to tell her story. Then she began abruptly:

"Yesterday, when you two girls mentioned Harold Norton's name, I became startled—almost frightened. You do not know that he has caused me much grief and unhappiness. It was really because of him and his unrelenting cruelty that I fled the country."

"Ex-Warden Norton is no friend of ours," Jean said encouragingly. "He has annoyed my sister several times."

Mrs. Keating, not hearing her, went on:

"My story goes back to a time before my marriage, when I was employed by a patent medicine manufacturing company. Harold Norton worked in the same department with me. Through mixed orders, I unwittingly put the wrong drug in a certain compound. Norton had labeled the medicines incorrectly; else the mistake would never have been made. As a result, the owner of the plant was sued by several people and forced to pay them heavy damages."

"I suppose you were discharged," Jean commented sympathetically, "and through no fault of your own."

Mrs. Keating shook her head.

"Of course, an investigation was started at the plant, and then I did a very foolish thing. Rather than face my questioners, I disappeared."

"But surely you could have made them understand how the mistake was made," Louise murmured.

"I don't know. I was very young at the time, and I fear somewhat of a coward. At any rate, I ran away. The next year I married, and in time almost forgot the dreadful incident. But Harold Norton learned of my whereabouts and made trouble for me."

"Surely he was as guilty as you were," Jean remarked indignantly.

"Yes, if he hadn't placed the wrong labels on the drugs I never should have made that mistake. However, the whole unfortunate episode haunted my thoughts day and night. I couldn't bear to think of my husband finding out about it. Harold Norton threatened to tell him everything unless I gave him money to keep quiet."

"Blackmail," Louise commented tersely.

"Yes. I made a great mistake when I gave him the first sum. He was never satisfied. He kept demanding more and more."

"And you were afraid to turn him over to the authorities," Jean murmured.

"At first I thought I would rather pay any amount than have the story come out. But Norton grew constantly more obnoxious. In recent years I am sure his mind has weakened. He threatened me until I didn't know which way to turn."

"I don't wonder that you grew desperate," Louise said.

"That was why I decided to burn down my house. I felt that if people thought I had perished in the flames, Harold Norton would not annoy me again. I would be free! Now you have my story."

The Dana girls had listened in amazement to this strange tale. It sounded almost incredible, yet they accepted it as the truth, for Mrs. Keating's words seemed sincere. They could not help but feel a genuine sympathy for the harassed woman. However, it appeared ridiculous to sacrifice Nina Regan's freedom because of Mrs. Keating's lack of courage.

"You must go to the authorities and repeat to them what you have just told us," Louise declared. "You owe it to Nina Regan to do so."

"And you should make some restitution to your former employer, or his heirs, even if it takes most of your money," Jean added.

"Then your conscience will be unclouded."

"Yes, you are right," the worried Mrs. Keating acknowledged in a low tone. "I never shall have any peace of mind until the whole matter is settled honorably."

"What was the name of your former employer?" Jean inquired.

"His name was Myron Brice. I doubt that he is still living after all these years."

The name electrified Jean and Louise. While it was a fairly common one, there was a strong possibility that Nina Regan's friend, Nellie Brice, was a relative of the former patent medicine manufacturer.

"If you'll give us complete data about your employer, we'll endeavor to learn just what became of him," Louise offered, trying to conceal her excitement.

Mrs. Keating told the girls all she knew regarding Mr. Brice. Louise and Jean then bade good-bye to the two women, and spent a busy hour at the telephone. From various sources they managed to glean scattered bits of information, until finally they were able to piece the entire story together. Then they hastened back to tell the harassed one what they had learned.

"It is amazing," Louise declared. "Your former employer, Mr. Brice, died a few years ago, and so did his son John."

"Then are there no heirs left?" Mrs. Keating questioned.

"I am coming to that. Mr. Brice's son had a wife named Nellie. She was wrongfully imprisoned, it seems, because of her husband's connection with a bank that failed."

"The employees of the Strong-Bone Medicine Company were heavy depositors in the institution," Jean added. "Strong sentiment was against Nellie because of that."

"And is this woman the only living member of the family?" Mrs. Keating asked.

"Yes, except a three-year-old crippled daughter," Louise answered.

"Mrs. Brice has had a most difficult time," Jean explained. "Since she has been in prison, her child hasn't had proper medical attention. Money would mean much to her."

"It seems that the family fortune ebbed away when the elder Mr. Brice paid out huge sums of money to the people who were made ill by taking doses of the erroneously labeled drug," Louise went on. "Then, when the bank failed, his son, who was alive at the time, and a heavy stockholder, gave the last of his property to help pay off depositors. Even with this sacrifice, many poor persons received nothing."

"Young Mr. Brice died shortly after the institution ceased to do business," Jean took up the story. "His wife Nellie, who also was a stockholder in the bank, was unjustly accused of falsifying its records to help out her husband. Authorities discovered that she was innocent of the charge only this week, when a cashier confessed to the felony.''

"Then Nellie will be allowed to go free," Mrs. Keating said in relief.

"Eventually, yes," Jean admitted. "But until all the depositors are paid, public sentiment will be against her as a large stockholder. But of course her stock is worthless and she has no money."

"What do you want me to do?" Mrs. Keating asked despairingly.

"You are a rich woman," Louise said quietly. "Unwittingly you have caused a great deal of trouble for both Nina Regan and Nellie Brice. It seems to me that you should make some kind of restitution."

"What can I do?"

"Give some of your money to Nellie Brice, with the understanding that she is to satisfy the bank judgment. In that way the employees of the Strong-Bone Medicine Company will recover their savings of a lifetime."

"How can I make amends to Nina?"

"By going with us to the authorities. When you have told them who you are, she will be given her freedom."

"That is the thing for you to do," Jean

urged. "As long as Nina Regan is imprisoned you will never have a moment's peace of mind."

"I know," Mrs. Keating murmured. She turned to her friend, Mrs. Zellow. "Tell me, Xenia, what shall I do?"

"That is for you to decide, my dear. However, it seems to me the plan the girls suggest is the happiest one for all concerned."

Mrs. Keating sat tense, gripping the arms of her chair. Her face was a study. Suddenly she relaxed somewhat her strained attitude and smiled at the Dana girls.

"You are right. I shall never have either happiness or assurance until I tell my story to the authorities. I will go with you whenever you like."

The Dana girls had not expected such an easy victory. They realized they had better hasten with Mrs. Keating to Pinecrest Reformatory before she might take a notion to change her decision.

"Can you be ready to start in half an hour?" Jean inquired.

"Yes, the sooner we leave the better."

Highly elated at their victory, Jean and Louise rushed out to meet Mrs. Grantland who was returning from church service.

They related to her all that had happened in the past hour.

"And you traced Mrs. Keating by using the breakfast trays as a clue!" Mrs. Grantland exclaimed in astonishment. "I never should have thought of that."

"Can you be ready to leave Crow's Point soon?" Jean queried eagerly.

"Yes. Now that Mrs. Keating is in a mood to confess everything, we should lose no time in getting her to Pinecrest."

Mrs. Grantland ordered her car sent to the door, and in less than half an hour the group had started for the reformatory. During the greater part of the ride Mrs. Keating sat tense beside Mrs. Zellow, saying very little.

"I shall be so glad when the ordeal is over," she remarked once.

When at last they reached the institution and Mrs. Selzer announced that the board of officials would see the party, Mrs. Keating began trembling. Jean and Mrs. Zellow supported her as they entered the conference room.

However, as the time came for the woman to tell her story, she grew calm. In a straightforward manner she related to the members of the governing body all she previously had told the Dana girls.

Jean and Louise were fearful lest the officials might not believe Mrs. Keating's strange tale, but to their relief the woman's word was never once questioned.

After hearing her story, the men conferred briefly among themselves, then requested Mrs. Selzer to bring Nina Regan into the room.

"I'll go after her at once," the matron smiled. "I'm so glad that at last she is to be free. I always felt that she was innocent."

Almost fifteen minutes elapsed before Mrs. Selzer returned alone. Her face revealed that something had gone amiss.

"Nina Regan has escaped again!" she told the startled group.

CHAPTER XXIV

A CRISIS

MRS. SELZER explained tersely to the board members just what had occurred. Less than twelve hours after her return to Pinecrest, Nina Regan had feigned illness and a doctor had ordered her to be taken to the infirmary. During the absence of a nurse she had managed to escape. No one had noticed that the young woman was missing until the matron visited the ward.

"It is certainly ironical that she ran away before finding out she had been exonerated," one of the board members commented regretfully.

"Shall I send out an alarm?" Mrs. Selzer questioned.

"I see no good reason for doing so," came the reply.

This decision was not entirely a pleasing one to the Dana girls. While it was true that Nina had gained her freedom, she would nevertheless be under the impression that the authorities were searching for her, and thus live in constant fear of being caught.

"Oh, Nina Regan must be told she is free!" Jean burst out.

"We can have her story printed in the papers and perhaps broadcast over the radio," the board member said, consenting. "Since Nina Regan is not actually guilty of a crime, the institution cannot afford to detail special officers to apprehend her."

Louise and Jean had no alternative but to be satisfied with the decision. However, they feared that Nina would never see the story in the newspaper, nor learn that she was free. They accordingly determined to take up the search for her themselves.

Mrs. Keating had expressed a desire to arrange a financial settlement with Nellie Brice. The young woman, already scheduled for release from the institution, was accordingly brought in.

At that moment Mrs. Keating's courage failed her, and she could not repeat her story to Nellie. When the Dana girls explained matters to her, the young woman delighted everyone by taking a very sensible attitude in the matter. She declared she was perfectly willing to accept whatever terms Jean and Louise might consider fair.

After an hour's deliberation, Mrs. Keating signed the necessary papers in the presence of a lawyer, transferring a generous amount of stocks, bonds, and property to Nellie Brice. Jean and Louise had fully expected the woman to collapse following the settlement, but instead she seemed greatly relieved.

"I feel better now than I have in months," she declared. "At last my conscience is clear."

"You will always be glad you righted the wrong, I feel sure," Mrs. Zellow told her kindly.

"Ex-Warden Norton will never be able to blackmail you again," Louise added. "And you still have enough money left to live comfortably for the rest of your days."

"I am through traveling for awhile," Mrs. Keating sighed. "It will seem good to stay at home once again."

Nellie Brice was a trifle dazed and bewildered at her good fortune, repeating over and over that the Dana girls were entirely responsible for the change wrought in her life.

"Just think, if I hadn't tried to give you that note to Pat Closky, you never would have known of me," she said, smiling. Turning to Mrs. Selzer, she added, "I hope you'll forgive me for acting the way I did while confined here at the institution."

"Certainly," the matron returned generously. "I don't wonder that you were upset all the time. I am sorry that you were ever held unjustly."

When she learned she was to be set free that very day, Nellie's first thought was for her crippled child.

"How is my little Carol?" she asked anxiously.

Mrs. Grantland reluctantly told her the unpleasant news. "Your child is in a hospital—" she began.

"Not seriously ill?" Nellie cried, interrupting the woman before she could finish her statement.

"Unfortunately, yes. However, when last we heard, she had rallied."

"Oh, my poor baby!" Nellie moaned. "Why wasn't I told about her before?"

Mrs. Selzer looked chagrined. As tactfully as possible the Dana girls then explained to Nellie why they had been unable to carry the news to her.

"When can I see my baby?" the mother implored.

"We'll take you to the hospital the instant you are released," Mrs. Grantland promised. "The doctors said that little Carol was in no immediate danger."

"We'll cut out all red tape and dismissal formalities, and you will be free to leave here in a few minutes," the chairman of the board told Nellie.

The necessary documents were hurriedly

signed. Nellie changed her prison garb for a tweed suit, and left Pinecrest Reformatory with Mrs. Grantland and the Dana girls. As the great iron doors closed behind her, Mrs. Brice breathed deeply. Tears came into her eyes.

"Free at last!" she whispered, stretching her arms upward. "Oh, you'll never know how wonderful it feels to be outdoors again, able to breathe the fresh air, and to see the world once more."

"Your life will be a happy one from this day on, I know," Louise told her.

"My only regret is that Nina Regan hasn't learned of her good fortune, too. Will the authorities be able to locate her soon, do you think?"

"I hope so," Louise answered.

She felt, however, that Nina would not be found before weeks of diligent search. Indisputably the young woman would employ every possible means to conceal her whereabouts from the authorities.

An hour's swift ride brought the group to the grounds of the Children's Hospital. As Mrs. Grantland and Nellie Brice were alighting from the car, Jean quietly drew her sister aside.

"Do you think the authorities will ever find Nina?" she asked her.

"I am afraid they won't, Jean."

"So am I. And she *must* be found."

"Perhaps she is right here at the hospital," Louise said unexpectedly.

"With Baby Carol, you mean? Do you think she would dare to come?"

"I believe Nina would take almost any risk just to be near the child. She loved that baby as much if it were her own."

"And she knew we were going to the reformatory to get Nellie when little Carol was so desperately ill," Jean added.

"If Nina isn't here, there's still another place where we might locate her."

"You're thinking of the hermitage?"

Louise nodded soberly. "As a last resort, we might look for her there. Let's hope we reach her before Ex-Warden Norton does."

"Norton!" Jean exclaimed. "I had almost forgotten about him."

"I am afraid he may try to make trouble when he finds out both Nellie and Nina have been released."

"That would be just like him," Jean agreed. "He may decide to take the law into his own hands."

"That's why we must lose no time in tracing Nina. She must be protected from that awful man," declared Louise.

The girls fell silent as Mrs. Grantland and

Nellie Brice joined them. Then they all went to the office of the Children's Hospital.

"How is Baby Brice feeling today?" the older woman inquired eagerly of the nurse at the information desk.

"You are Mrs. Grantland, aren't you?"

"Yes. What news can you give us? We have brought the child's mother at last."

The nurse arose, and her kind eyes met those of Nellie.

"Tell me the truth," the young woman urged courageously. "Only tell it to me quickly."

"Baby Brice is in the operating room now," the nurse said quietly. "Her life hangs on a slender thread."

"Is there a chance?"

"A chance? Yes."

"May I see my baby now?"

The nurse shook her head, and taking Nellie gently by the arm, led her to a nearby couch.

"Several hours must elapse before we can be sure of the outcome of the operation. Until then, try to get some rest."

"There were sure to be," said she, and the older girl had given a long breath of relief.
...

CHAPTER XXV

NINA'S HAVEN

LOUISE and Jean remained in the lobby of the hospital until word was sent down to them that Baby Carol had been taken from the operating room.

"She is still under the anesthetic," the nurse told the anxious little group. "It is too early to state definitely whether or not she will rally."

During the long wait the Dana girls had made several inquiries, but were told that Nina Regan had not as yet visited the hospital.

"Now that Baby Carol is in such grave danger it is imperative that we locate her," Jean whispered to her sister.

"Yes, if the child should die, Nina would never get over not having seen her."

"We can do no good by staying here, Louise. Why not ask Mrs. Grantland if we can use her car to drive over to the hermitage? Perhaps Nina is there."

The plan appealed to Louise. When they spoke of it to Mrs. Grantland, she readily turned over her automobile keys to them.

"I'll stay here with Nellie," she told the girls. "If you find Nina, bring her straight to the hospital."

Without adventure or mishap, the Dana girls drove to Clairtown and on toward the hermitage. They parked on a side road and hiked through the woods. As they emerged from among the trees, Louise, who was in the lead, abruptly halted.

"What is it?" Jean demanded.

Then she saw for herself. Harold Norton was standing at the cave entrance of the hermitage, talking to someone inside. The girls guessed at once that it was Nina Regan.

"Come out, or I'll wall you in," they heard the man shout angrily. "Come out, I say!"

The Danas were too far away to catch Nina's reply. However, it stunned them as they saw Norton start to carry out his threat. He began gathering several rocks, which he piled up one above the other over the only exit of the wrecked cabin.

"The villain is burying her alive!" Jean exclaimed.

She started forward, but Louise placed a restraining hand on her sister's arm.

"Don't you know he has a revolver, Jean?"

"But we can't stand here and let him bury Nina!"

"Of course not, but I know a better plan."

Louise then led her sister back to the parked car, where they found a heavy auto robe which had been left in the rear seat. Carrying the blanket, they quietly slipped up behind Norton. He was so engrossed in his cruel work of sealing Nina within her tomb that he did not hear their approaching footsteps.

Without warning, the Dana girls threw the robe over the man's head, completely befuddling him. He struggled violently to free himself, but they wound the heavy coverlet tightly about him.

"Now we'll see how *you* enjoy having the tables turned," Louise said.

They hastily sealed the cruel fellow into one of the cave-like rooms of the hermitage, completely ignoring his smothered pleas to escape. Then they called to the prisoner.

"Come on out!" Jean called. "Everything's safe!"

Like a trapped animal, the young woman bolted from within. She bestowed one terrified glance upon Louise and Jean; then turning, she ran as fast as she could toward the forest.

"She thinks we intend to take her back to the reformatory," Louise cried. "We must stop her."

They hurried after the fleeing figure, calling to her, and trying to make her understand that their motive was a friendly one. At last Nina understood. With a sigh of relief she sank down on a log to wait for them.

"We only came to tell you that you are free," Louise said, catching her breath. "Mrs. Keating has been found. She has confessed everything, and has exonerated you entirely."

Nina sprang to her feet, her eyes alight with happiness.

"Oh, I knew that some day the truth would come out!" Then her face clouded. "But are you sure?"

"Absolutely," Jean smiled.

"Harold Norton is still pursuing me, and found me here today. I tried to outwit him, but he avenged himself by burying me alive in the hermitage. If you girls hadn't arrived just when you did, I surely should have perished."

"Warden Norton will never trouble you again," Louise promised.

From the forest the three could hear the man's muffled shouts. At length Jean and Louise relented, and released him from his prison. The ordeal had left him a changed, broken man.

"You're going to hear just what we have to say," Jean told him severely. "Then, unless you agree to do exactly as we tell you, you'll be ending your days in some prison."

The Dana girls had taken the precaution to secure the man's revolver, but that was hardly necessary. He had lost his fight. He seemed to be years older.

"What is it you want me to do?" he muttered.

Louise and Jean related the story of their meeting with Mrs. Keating. When Norton learned that he had been implicated in the woman's confession, he became as putty in the hands of the two clever sisters.

"You must leave this section of the country at once and never return unless you want to be taken prisoner," Jean ended her talk severely. "As it is, we're letting you off easier than you deserve to be."

"In case you don't know it, you're taking the next cross continent train," Louise added. "And we'll accompany you to the station ourselves."

Norton made no protest as they led him to the automobile. At Clairtown the girls learned that an express would arrive in a few minutes. Taking money they found in the ex-warden's wallet, they purchased a ticket to the farthest point.

"Remember, you must never come back," Jean cautioned, as he boarded the express.

Norton disappeared into a day coach, and a minute later the train pulled out of the station. That was the last the Dana girls were ever to see of him; nor did he return again to trouble Nina Regan.

"Well, that's the end of that episode," Louise remarked in relief as the group went back to the automobile.

Nina's joy over her release from the reformatory gave way to a feeling of grief when she learned that Baby Brice was in grave danger. She urged the Dana girls to take her to the hospital as quickly as possible.

Before they had traveled very far, Jean and Louise noted that their supply of gasoline was running low, and stopped at the first station. While an attendant was filling up the tank, Jean slipped into the office to make a telephone call. She was fairly beaming when she returned to the car, but refused to explain the reason for her looking so pleased.

When they arrived at the hospital, the three were met by Mrs. Grantland and Nellie Brice. One glance at their relieved faces told them that Baby Carol was out of danger.

"The doctors say she will live," Nellie declared happily. "And they think she has a very good chance of walking normally in a few years."

At her first opportunity, Jean drew Nina Regan aside.

"You must phone Fred Lester," she in-

sisted. "He will be interested to hear of your
release."

"I haven't seen him for so long I doubt that
he still cares for me."

"I feel sure he does; in fact, I talked to him
only a few minutes ago and hinted that I might
have some good news for him soon."

"Then I'll call him up," Nina agreed.
"Only I'm almost afraid to do it for fear he
might have changed in his feeling toward me."

The Dana girls escorted her to a phone, and
waited outside the booth for nearly half an
hour.

"I didn't mean to take such a long time,"
Nina apologized as she emerged. "We had
so much to say to each other."

"I am glad everything is all right," Louise
smiled.

She could read Nina's happiness in her eyes.
A tell-tale flush crept slowly over the young
woman's face; then she laughed at being so
flustered.

"Fred is leaving his work at once and coming here to the hospital to get me," she confessed. "I guess Jean was right. He hasn't
changed at all in his feeling toward me."

"Didn't I tell you!" the blonde Dana cried
triumphantly.

In less than an hour the young man arrived.
He and Nina were seen wandering about the

grounds of the institution together. A little later Nina sought out the Dana girls to show them a beautiful diamond engagement ring she was wearing.

"It's the one I returned to Fred so long ago," she explained. "He has kept it all these months."

It was inevitable that Louise and Jean should receive a great deal of praise for the efficient manner in which they had aided both Nellie Brice and Nina Regan. They excused themselves, however, by declaring that they must hasten back to Starhurst.

The modesty of the sisters in taking credit was outstanding. This could be noted especially in their next adventure with "The Circle of Footprints."

"Tell us everything about the hermitage case," begged one of their classmates when the sisters had returned to school and many of their friends had gathered in the Dana suite to hear the story.

"The whole thing really started when I stumbled into the well," Louise laughed. "From the time of my first visit there, I just felt that old hermitage guarded some deep and mysterious secret. Jean and I couldn't be satisfied until we had delved into it."

With the exception of Lettie Briggs and Ina Mason, no one begrudged the Dana girls their

bright place in the limelight. The two dis-
gruntled ones withdrew from their classmates,
circulating throughout the school the conten-
tion that there were few students at Starhurst
worth cultivating.

"Perhaps Ellen Symington, who is coming
here next term, will be more to your liking,"
Jean jokingly remarked a few days later.

This comment had the effect of stirring Lettie into renewed activity. Secretly she took it
upon herself to delve closely into Ellen Symington's genealogy to find out if she would
make a "suitable" companion. Since the Dana
girls were indirectly responsible for her coming to Starhurst, the vindictive Lettie hoped
that she might perhaps unearth some scandal
which would discredit the newcomer in the eyes
of the school. Greatly to her annoyance, she
learned through extensive research that the
Symington family was an old and honorable
one.

Another fact which she gleaned was even
more provoking: Nina Regan was a cousin of
the famous art collector from abroad, Harvey
Symington! Lettie fully intended to keep this
information a secret, but in an unguarded moment forgot herself and blurted it out to Louise
and Jean.

"How wonderful!" Louise cried in delight.
"That shows that Nina has inherited her talent

for sculpturing—that it is in her very blood."

To Lettie's discomfiture, the Dana girls rushed off to Penfield to tell Nina the good news. They found her at Mrs. Grantland's home where she was spending several days.

"I've already had more happiness than I deserve," the young woman declared on hearing of her relative. "I'll never be able to repay you girls for all the wonderful things you have done for me."

"There's one way in which you can, Nina," Jean said, her eyes sparkling. "Make us a model of the hermitage! It will serve to remind us of the thrilling adventure we've shared."

"It has been thrilling, hasn't it?" Louise sighed. "I almost wish it hadn't ended."

But Louise and Jean soon were to have another adventure, equally exciting, when they encountered the mysterious "Circle of Footprints."